Something ab...
got to him.

Gloria Pellman look... gently. Yet she faced adversity with fire and fury and a sweetly stubborn chin.

She wasn't much to look at. Skinny.

But the first time Hank touched her, he was ready to defend her to the death. And when he'd held her briefly in his arms, he'd felt more than capable of slaying dragons.

Hank snorted softly. He might be attracted, but he wasn't stupid. It must have been the way Glorie's body fit so perfectly with his that had temporarily blown away his common sense.

Well, he had it back now.

This scrappy single mum, with her nothing looks and her solemn, wide-eyed little son, was nothing but trouble.

And Hank vowed to steer clear of both of them...

Dear Reader,

Travel to the heat of Arizona with us this month and discover the mysteries of Cherokee Erin Wolf, our July THAT SPECIAL WOMAN! from perennially popular writer Lindsay McKenna. Or you could head west with Anne McAllister and find out what could possibly cause *A Cowboy's Tears*. It's worth the trip...

Penny Richards has written the first book in an interesting mini-series about four men...SWITCHED AT BIRTH. Look out for the other stories over the next three months—only in Special Edition. And then there's *Husband: Bought and Paid For* by Laurie Paige that delivers just what it promises—a wonderful marriage of convenience story.

There's also a fun-filled first Special Edition from Judy Christenberry and an emotional debut for Doris Rangel. They're all great reading and we hope you'll love them!

The Editors

Mountain Man
DORIS RANGEL

SILHOUETTE

SPECIAL EDITION

First published in Great Britain 1998
Silhouette Books, Eton House, 18-24 Paradise Road,
Richmond, Surrey TW9 1SR

© Doris Rangel 1997

ISBN 0 373 24140 2

23-9807

Printed and bound in Spain
by Litografía Rosés S.A., Barcelona

Thanks, Dad.

DORIS RANGEL

loves books...the feel of them, the smell of them, the sight of them. And she loves talking about them. She has collected them, organized them, sold them new and used, written them, taught others to write them, read them aloud to children and published them. History, philosophy, science, satire, Western, romance...she loves reading it all. In her home, books are the wallpaper of choice.

B.C. (Before Children), Doris worked for the Peace Corps in the Philippines and was bitten by the dreaded travel bug. Since then, she's been prone to abandoning her three grown or nearly grown urchins in order to wander the roads of mediaeval Japan, Regency England or modern Australia, all for the price of a paperback. What a bargain! But she admits someday she hopes to breathe in the frigid air of Antarctica first-hand, and personally traverse a hanging walkway among the treetops in a rain forest. Someday. In the meantime, her fictional characters do the wandering, little knowing they carry her piggyback.

If readers have comments concerning her books, Doris would love to hear from them. Her address is P.O. Box 5645, Victoria, TX 77903-5645, USA.

All underlined places are fictitious.

Chapter One

The eagle hung motionless, the only living thing in a vast cloudless sky. It rose and fell, riding gentle swells of air current beneath its wings, its attention never wavering from the desert floor hundreds of feet below.

It had no interest in the man who sat on the edge of the sheer cliff only a little below its own altitude, an arm resting on the bent knee of one leg, the other leg hanging over the cliff and dangling into space.

A part of the environment, the man was as still as the surrounding boulders. Only the light breeze gave him the illusion of movement, ruffling the thick straight hair that glinted blue-black in the thin mountain sunlight. His eyes were as hard and relentless as the eagle's, and black as winter rain.

Suddenly the giant bird plummeted to the desert valley far below, falling with unerring accuracy onto a rabbit that moved from its meager cover. Then, with the animal clutched in its talons, the strong beat of widespread wings sent the magnificent bird upward once more where it quickly disappeared behind the wall of rocks and trees, shielding its aerie from prying eyes.

The man remained silent until the sky emptied of movement, then spoke to the limitless space before him.

"What do you want, kid? Are you lost?"

Jamey jumped, startled. The man sat sideways on the cliff edge but faced away from the boy's hiding place. Even so the child crouched lower against his tree and swallowed convulsively, unable to answer.

Though he hadn't raised his voice, the man's tone clearly held irritation…and Jamey knew better than to cause any man irritation.

Slowly the man's head turned toward him and he cowered lower, trying to blend his small person into the trees and shrubbery.

"If you want to hide, kid, don't wear a red shirt. Now are you going to tell me what you want? I didn't come here for company."

As unerringly as the eagle's, the hard black eyes pinned him to his tree. Trembling, Jamey stood, to stare back as intently as the man stared at him. The man's face might have been carved by the same hand that carved the mountain. It was similarly uncompromising and linear, eyes hidden in twin caverns between high angled cheekbones and brows. The only touch of softness came from luxuriant lashes that should have been out of place but somehow were not.

Jamey swallowed again, certainly not trusting the

hint of gentleness in those lashes. Yet he had no choice.

Rubbing the back of a grubby hand under his nose in a nervous gesture, he straightened his thin shoulders. "It's my mama. She fell and…and she won't get up."

The man had been sitting. In a blur of movement he stood on his feet. Jamey blinked.

"Where is she?"

"Over there." He waved a vague arm. "Near a ditch. There's two trees standing real close together, but one of them's broken."

"I know the place. Let's go."

As the man walked away from the face of the cliff, the edge where he had been sitting shifted infinitesimally, a small fissure opening in the rocky surface.

For a long second the earth seemed to hold its breath before the edge pulled away. It slipped, hung suspended for a micromoment of eternity, then fell slowly down the steep walls to gather speed, rocks and debris. With a muted roar it tumbled to the valley far below.

At last the earth let go a soundless sigh and a small bird trilled to its mate somewhere in the pines.

The man merely lifted a sardonic brow, but Jamey was shocked by the small disappearance of earth before his eyes.

"Just a little rock slide, boy."

Immediately the man moved toward the trees and Jamey fell silently in behind him. Soon he trotted, the pace set not taking into account his short legs. Though the man's stride held no sense of hurry, in no time they had followed the ravine to the spot where his mother lay, white and unmoving.

To an experienced woodsman the signs telling the brief story were clear. The woman had stepped on a branch that rolled under her foot, sending her crashing to the earth on her back. A stone was obviously hidden somewhere in the thick carpet of pine needles. She was out cold, a complication Hank wanted like he wanted World War Three.

Brown pine needles clung to the mass of lank black hair and to the faded yellow sweater she wore buttoned up as a blouse with her jeans. Her bloodless face gave an alabaster quality to tawny skin stretched tightly across prominent cheekbones, defining pronounced hollows in her face. She had a short nose, but it was high-bridged and thinly aristocratic. It was a face full of character, but not pretty.

"Well, you don't have to fight the men off," he muttered, bending over the unconscious woman and running quick fingers over the small bones of her slender body. "You're too damned thin. Don't you women ever learn?" No broken bones, however. Gently he pushed his fingers through the rough, thickly curling hair and over the delicately rounded skull until he located the wound. No blood, but a good-size goose egg.

He couldn't leave her. By the time he drove to Tulaca, located the doctor and brought him back here, the sun would be gone. Doc Wilson, short and rotund, wouldn't thank him for a walk through the timber in the dark.

"What's your name, kid?" Hank threw the question back to the boy standing silently at his shoulder.

The boy's golden brown eyes were dry, but fear shone in them clearly. "James Pellman, sir. Is my mama dead?"

He's too damned thin, too, Hank thought briefly. "No, she's not dead. Just unconscious. Hit her head on a rock."

The words made no attempt to comfort, yet they seemed to give the boy courage. "I'm going to take her to my cabin, Jim," he said abruptly. "But first I'll try to wake her up."

Easy to say, Hank thought grimly. If this was a man, he'd just slap his face around a bit and let nature do the rest. He forced himself to pat the woman's thin cheeks with gentle precision instead.

She gave a soft moan, then stilled.

Hank gazed at the quiet face in frustration before sitting back to rethink the situation and come up with Plan B. Wearing the sweater buttoned up to her neck as she did, perhaps she couldn't get enough air, he decided.

"So I'll unbutton a couple of buttons," he muttered to himself, and almost smiled because the boy, watching the proceedings with cautious interest, nodded in grave agreement.

Reaching out, Hank released the top button of the sweater, fumbling a little, feeling strangely all thumbs. Angry at this unprecedented nervousness, he undid the second, concentrating on his hands. When she groaned again softly, he knew he was making progress.

"Third one's the charm," he told the boy triumphantly…and caught a blow to the side of his head that set his ears ringing.

Why, the ungrateful fool of a woman had *hit* him!

He was so surprised that only by reflex did he catch her arms as she sat halfway up to hit him again.

"Hey, now. None of that. I'm the good guy!"

Bringing her two arms together in front of her so that both thin wrists were held in one of his hands, his other hand caught her face under her chin and over her throat as she began butting him in the chest. Beside him, he heard the boy murmur in distress.

The woman's eyes were the same golden brown as her son's, only where the boy's lashes were blond, hers were dark, thick, and straight.

And now those golden eyes shot fire at him as she ordered outrageously, "T-take your hands off m-me." Her chin pushed against his hand with all the aggressiveness of a banty hen as she tried without success to stick it out.

Just as if *she's* the one with the upper hand, Hank thought in amazement.

And she was scared to death.

The realization came from nowhere and he swallowed in an effort to clear his features, knowing after years of experience just how intimidating his rough-hewn face could be to someone not used to it.

Trying his best to look reassuring, he smiled at her, dropped her wrists, and reflexively reached to smooth the wild rough mass of her hair as one might an anxious child's. She had enough of it to have been more than adequately padded when she hit the rock. "Nothing to you but eyes and hair, is there?" he murmured, adding, "You have a head wound, ma'am. I can't let you toss yourself around, now can I?"

Who *is* this man? Gloria thought dazedly. Her head hurt and the man was touching her. *Touching* her! Frantic, she began to struggle.

"Ah, hell!" Hank growled disgustedly. "Lady, stop jumping around like that. You're going to hurt yourself. I'll leave you alone. Just be still, you hear me? *Be still!*"

But the woman was apparently beyond listening. Left with no alternative, Hank pulled the slight body forward into an encompassing hug that held her torso close enough to his own that her flailing arms were free but the blows she tried to land ineffectual. By burying his chin over the back of one of her thin shoulders, he kept his head out of hitting range and her head reasonably immobile. In such a position she merely wasted energy and did little harm to either of them.

He saw, however, that the boy was frightened silly, all but wringing his hands and dancing from one foot to the other. There wasn't a damn thing Hank could do about it, though, on his knees as he was and clutching a hysterical woman who wanted to tear his head off. Almost by accident, he caught Jim's gaze, rolled his own eyes helplessly in silent apology, and managed a small shrug.

The boy blinked, and stilled, mouth agape.

Hank smiled.

And Jim almost smiled back, but not quite.

Gradually, as he had known it would, the woman's flailing became sporadic, finally stopping altogether. Her arms hung limply over his and her forehead drooped forward as if she were just too tired to hold it up any longer. The only place for it to go was to his shoulder. Pressed near his own, her heart tattooed as rapidly as a windup monkey's cymbals.

Though she lay loosely against him, he felt a fine tension running through her.

Over her shoulder Hank smiled again to himself, but he didn't release her from his protective embrace.

"You're scaring your boy, you know," he said conversationally. "Jim's standing right here thinking you're wanting to murder me."

She turned her head slowly to check his words and Jamey looked back at her, his escalating panic obvious. He's right, Gloria thought. I'm scaring Jamey and I'm being silly. Automatically, she fought the acknowledgment of how good the protective arms felt around her, and instead pulled into her mind her stubborn belief in her own strength. But just for a moment she let herself relax…

Hank felt the woman's heartbeat gradually slow to steadiness. When she didn't speak, he, too, remained silent. At last she gave a small tired sigh.

"I'm going to let you go now," he said softly into her hair. "But first I'm warning you not to hit me again. I mean you no harm and you have no cause to fight me."

In spite of his words he didn't release her and she didn't struggle. Her head fit into his shoulder just below his ear and he felt her warm breath on his neck. When he raised his head from behind her shoulder she didn't stir.

"I wasn't trying anything," he explained with a touch of unusual awkwardness. For some damn reason this woman completely disconcerted him. Again he smoothed the back of her hair with his hand. "I only loosened your sweater so you could breathe."

But was he explaining to her or to himself? Hell, he wasn't used to explaining himself to anybody and couldn't say he liked the feeling, either.

The woman in his arms brought the situation to a much needed halt.

At his words, she lifted her head abruptly, the back

of her head knocking painfully against his ear. "I'm all right now," she said, and jerked away from him so that his arms fell away from her.

And she was, too, Gloria told herself. Oh, she'd been scared there for a minute, but not now. This man, for all his rough face, didn't really scare her in the least. Her chin unconsciously thrust itself forward into battle position.

Hoity-toity, Hank thought. No thank-you. No gratitude. No nothing. Not that he expected it.

"You're probably just fine," he acknowledged, his voice now as cold as hers. "But you took a nasty fall and knocked yourself out for a few minutes. Someone who knows more about it than you or I needs to examine your head. They can't do it here."

She stiffened. "I don't need my head examined. I'm perfectly all right." Awkwardly, she stood...and wobbled dangerously.

"Yeah, I can see that." Hank scooped her into his arms without giving her a chance to argue further. Tiresome woman.

Again he set off through the trees, the boy trotting behind. The woman struggled briefly, then subsided. Perhaps she, too, thought there were better places to argue.

To Jamey, the man striding in front of him was...awfully big. And tall. The muscles of his calves and thighs molded the faded jeans as his long legs ate up the distance.

There were no excesses about him, no extra layers of fat on his body, no unneeded motions to his movement, no unnecessary words in his speech. His very silence and economy of movement made Jamey feel protected. This silent man could and would take care of things.

They came to a dirt road, the same one he and his mama had trod earlier, and walked down it in the direction of the town at the foot of the mountain. A cabin sat in a small meadow off to the side of the road, showing no sign of life—no smoke came from its rock chimney and the front door stood closed against intruders. His mama had said it looked lonely.

Inside, the cabin was as spare and economical as its owner, with only one room doing duty as living room, bedroom and kitchen. Jamey's eyes passed over the sparse furnishings. A bed stood in a corner with a small chest of drawers near it. A stove and refrigerator took up one short wall, fronted by a table with two chairs. A comfortable-looking recliner sat near the fireplace. Nothing else…no ornaments, no spread on the bed or cloth on the table, no curtains at the windows, no rugs on the floor. Only the books filling cases reaching floor to ceiling lessened its austerity.

"Pull the blankets back on the bed, kid."

Predictably, the woman jerked and began a frantic struggling so that Hank almost dropped her.

"Oh, for Pete's sake!" he exploded impatiently, and dumped her, not as gently as he probably should have, on the side of the bed before the boy could pull back the blanket.

She promptly tried to jump off again but by this time Hank had had enough. "Sit down," he said ominously, "or so help me I'm going to get good and mad. You are overreacting."

Though she immediately stilled, Hank knew that

any second she was going to come off the bed like a small tornado. More important, the boy had gone white. Damn. With his face, Hank knew he shouldn't have lost his temper.

He wasn't about to let his remorse show, however, but rapped out, "Jim, get up on the bed with your mother and hold her hand. I think she's scared," and came close to laughing aloud when the woman looked completely affronted. But with her son sitting beside her, his hand tucked in hers, she seemed to relax slightly.

Hank took advantage of the shaky truce and backed off a few feet, thrusting his hands into his back pockets.

"Now," he said. "Lady, you've fallen and banged your head. It needs looking at and I need—"

"Gloria," she said tersely.

He nodded. "Gloria. I need to know if someone's on the mountain looking for you. They're probably worried."

She opened her mouth, but hesitated.

Why am I not surprised? Hank thought cynically. She's going to lie even when the truth is to her advantage.

"No one's on the mountain," she said. "But my husband is waiting for me at home. He knew where Jamey and I were going and will be expecting us back any moment now."

She was lying. But he had to acknowledge that if he wanted to harm her, a husband waiting might make him think twice. It was a shame to burst her bubble.

Hank nodded as if he believed her. "I'm going after Doc Wilson. He's one of the few doctors left who still does house calls. Until he says it's okay, I don't want to move you any more than necessary and it's a rough ride into town. After I pick the doc up, I'll swing by and get your husband and bring him back here with us. Where do you live?''

Golden eyes glinted at him with malevolence. ''Why don't you just telephone the doctor?'' she asked suspiciously.

Hank rubbed a hand over his mouth to hide his grin. ''I don't have a telephone.''

The woman's chin lifted and her eyes narrowed. With her delicate hawk's nose and her wild black hair that still had bracken in it from her fall, she looked like tribal royalty who was not amused. ''I live at five-oh-three Madison,'' she said. ''Should my husband already be on his way to look for me, please tell one of the neighbors where I am.''

Five-oh-three Madison. So the house was rented again. ''What's your husband's name?'' he asked wearily, all desire for laughter having fled.

She sidestepped with neat efficiency. ''Pellman is our last name,'' she said.

''Right. Well, Ms. Gloria Pellman, I'm going after the doc. I suggest you sit still, not eat anything, but stay awake. If the boy is hungry, he can raid the refrigerator. I'll be back as soon as I can.''

Before Gloria could think of a thing to add, the man was gone. She stared speechlessly at the closed cabin door as she heard a car motor come to life and then the low, diminishing hum of the automobile as it left for town.

She turned to look at Jamey, who silently looked back at her. Then she left the bed and walked swiftly to the door. When she twisted the knob, the door swung silently open.

He was right, she thought, staring out into the late afternoon sunshine. I overreacted. I acted as if a man who was only trying to help an injured hiker was Jack the Rapist.

Resting her throbbing head against the edge of the thick wooden door, she sighed. It was the first day of the new life she'd blithely promised herself and Jamey. And after coming to Tulaca to leave her past behind, at the first innocent helping hand she'd resurrected that past all over again.

"Mama?" Jamey's soft voice claimed her attention.

Gloria lifted her head from the door and turned to him with a smile. "We can leave anytime we want, sweetie. Shall we go home?" Her heart softened at the sound of the word and all it had come to mean to her and her son.

But surprisingly, Jamey didn't move from his perch. "He's coming back, Mama." The statement wasn't made in fear, but as a reminder. Another surprise.

Walking back to the bed, Gloria sat down again beside the boy and put an arm around his thin shoulders. "And bringing a doctor with him. I suppose it would be rude to leave after he's gone to so much trouble."

Jamey huddled into her embrace. "Will he bring Daddy?" he whispered, and she felt him tremble.

Tipping his chin up, she gazed steadily into the tawny eyes so like her own. "Daddy's dead, Jamey. He doesn't live on this earth anymore. I thought you understood that." Wrapping him in both arms, Gloria hugged her son comfortingly.

But how can a five-year-old understand death? she thought. Even though he'd gone to his father's funeral, Jamey still expected Eric to pop from behind every bush.

In an effort to distract him, she asked lightly, "Are you hungry?" but he shook his head. Nestling further into her arms, he sighed. Tired, his body language said, and she knew that if she sat still much longer Jamey would be asleep.

She shook him a little and stood. "Let's get your shoes off and you can lie down awhile until the man gets back."

The man, she thought, and grimaced. It sounded like a title. "What's his name, do you know?" she asked Jamey as she untied his shoe laces, but Jamey shook his head.

Pulling back the army-issue wool blanket to reveal pristine white sheets, Gloria had Jamey crawl in to nestle onto one of the feather pillows.

Feather pillows, she thought in amazement, in this one-room cabin without a hint of softness in it!

Within moments Jamey slept, looking so comfortable that she decided to lie down beside him for a few minutes herself.

Drifting into sleep, a cynical smile curved her lips. *The man,* she thought drowsily.

"Damn." The curse, while quiet, was emphatic enough to swirl like blue smoke through the stillness of the car. The doctor was out, fighting a flu epidemic spreading rapidly through the area. His wife had no idea when or if he would make it in but agreed with

Hank that the woman shouldn't be moved. She also gave him a pamphlet on concussion. One of the precautions recommended was continuous observation for at least twenty-four hours.

"And that's a hell of a beginning to my vacation," Hank groused aloud.

The past six months had been particularly grueling. The negotiations with the Japanese for linking F & M Trucking with Japanese harbors in Mexico to transport goods into the United States had been a nightmare all by itself. It had taken a mini-United Nations' summit to pull that one off without offending anyone, including his suspicious American employees who were fearful of seeing their jobs go out of the country.

Then there had been the railroad car full of automobile parts, loaded in Akron and bound for Tulsa, that disappeared into thin air days before the opening of a new franchise dealership. The car resurfaced two weeks later on a sidetrack in Texarkana, of all places, but the two weeks it had been missing had made neither him nor his employees very happy. The fact that several employees of MidContinent Railroad, blue-collar as well as some very white-collar, were now not quite so happy, either, only mildly relieved the initial frustration.

Yet those were the larger problems, and possibly the most minor. He knew that it was the nit-picking day-to-day crises that drove one up the wall. And Hank was well and truly up the wall, to the point where it was get out of Albuquerque or have his office staff rebel.

Nor did it help that for the past year he'd been asking himself just why the hell he was beating his brains out anyway. He had all the money he needed. As the cliché said, he could only wear one pair of pants at a time...or drive one car or visit one European capital at a time, for that matter. The thrill of the hunt had died long ago and he was tired. Damn tired. And now he had a hysterical hiker and her big-eyed kid on his hands. Another nit-picking problem.

Hank backed the classic '56 Chevrolet out of the drive beside the doctor's house, drove slowly to the short main street of Tulaca, then angled down another side street that took him to five-oh-three Madison.

The small dingy house sat neglected and silent in the early twilight, its front door closed, no vehicle in the drive.

Getting out of the car, Hank stared at the bleak facade a moment before striding up to the front door. He knew no one was home, but his conscience wouldn't let him not go by the house at all. He gave a token series of thuds on the front door but didn't even bother listening for an answer. Pulling a deposit slip out of his checkbook, he scribbled a note on the back of it, stuck it in the screen, then cut across the weedy lawn to the neighbor's.

Melanie Hensley came to the door. "Hank!" she exclaimed in surprise.

"Hi, Melanie. No, I'm not coming in. This isn't a social call. You have new neighbors, the Pellmans. The wife was hurt on the mountain and is at my cabin. Inform her husband, would you, when he gets in?"

"Why, I didn't see anyone over there," Melanie said, frowning. "I have both Frankie and Big Frank down with the stomach flu so I've been pretty busy.

It's all over town, you know. But, I'll tell her husband if I see him.''

"Thanks, Melanie. Don't worry if you miss him. I left a note on the screen. Tell Frank and Frankie I hope they're feeling better soon. I'm here for a while so I'll probably see you around.'' And he left, knowing that tidbit of information would be all over town by tomorrow, as well.

He took the mountain road at sixty, the Chevy purring over the rough mountain road and riding smooth and even, its power strongly leashed but begging for release. As Hank slowed for the switchback curves that led ever upward, his bad mood escalated with the altitude.

Ordinarily, he wouldn't have bothered with the kid, but this one had seemed sort of lost and frightened and too small to be looking that way.

And where was Gloria Pellman's man? There had to be one. She had that look about her, the one that said there was a man in the background somewhere. But with that chip on her shoulder, the background was probably where she wanted him to stay. The boy hadn't said anything about his dad, but then the boy had acted scared witless.

He hadn't cried though, scared as he was, Hank added to himself with a touch of reluctant admiraion.

And he couldn't help but wonder how the two had come to be on the mountain in the first place. They sure as hell didn't drop from the sky—not in those clothes. The kid was just short of ragged in his faded shirt with the sleeves riding tight on the shoulders.

Nor was his mother dressed any better. Those sandals, for example. There was nothing to the thin, cheap things. No wonder she'd taken a tumble. The silly woman should've known better.

Hank turned into the rutted drive through the meadow, parking next to the cabin. No lights showed, though the sun was down enough to make the interior of the cabin gloomy. Maybe she'd taken her boy and left, or the mysterious husband had come for them. He liked that idea.

The front door stood ajar, however. As he pushed open the screen, Hank reached out and flipped a switch on the inside wall near the door to turn on a lamp beside the recliner.

"Damn."

Gloria Pellman lay in his bed fast asleep, the boy beside her asleep, also, curled up on the other pillow. He'd let the boy sleep, but Hank knew he had to wake the mother. According to the pamphlet, drowsiness was not a good sign.

Absently, he reached over and pulled the rough army blanket over the sleeping boy, his eyes never leaving the mother's quiet face. She looked worn out. It seemed a shame to wake her only to ask how she was feeling.

He allowed his large hand to smooth the tangled hair. For some reason it fascinated him and he brushed it away from the thin aristocratic face. By some unexplained alchemy, with the touch of the rough strands beneath his palms, his anger, impatience, and frustration with this interruption to his longed-for solitude disappeared.

The thought ignited a brief anger before he sighed and turned away from the bed.

Nights were cold on the mountain and there was already a chill in the cabin. Perhaps he should build a fire. Sure as hell, what peace existed in the room now was going to fly straight out the window just as soon as the bed's occupant was awake and verbal again.

Wasn't a crackling fire reputed to have a calming effect?

A hand shook her shoulder gently but insistently. Gloria shrugged it off in irritation. She was in a sweet-smelling meadow with a touch of woodsmoke hanging in the air, and more comfortable than she'd been in weeks. Whoever was bothering her could just go away.

"Mrs. Pellman."

She hunched her shoulder and snuggled further into the surrounding softness.

"Mrs. Pellman." A little worry now in the low rumbling voice with its hint of drawl.

"Gloria."

"What?" She sat up abruptly, only to gaze around her in confusion. Where was her grassy meadow? Turning to the hard-faced, black-eyed man who had been bending over her and with whom she'd almost knocked heads, she asked accusingly, "What am I doing here?"

"Confusion," she heard him mutter as he eyed her warily. "I brought you to my cabin after you fell," he said aloud. "Don't you remember?"

She blinked, then touched the back of her sore head gingerly. "Yes, of course. Sorry."

The man had taken several steps away from the bed and now gazed at her as if she had a contagious disease. Did she need deodorant?

"You were going to bring the doctor," she reminded him suspiciously when she found no one else in the room.

"Uh, yeah. But there's a flu epidemic in Tulaca and the doc was out. His wife didn't know when he'd be back but she gave me a pamphlet on concussion."

As if to verify his words, he pulled a folded brochure from his back jeans' pocket and held it up.

Gloria threw off the blanket and swung her legs over the side of the bed. "I don't have a concussion," she said briskly, her eyes searching the floor for her sandals.

A large hand on her shoulder effectively anchored her to the bed.

Her head jerked up. "Take your hand off me." The words came out a vicious hiss and she poised to spring.

The black eyes boring into hers didn't so much as blink, but the man removed his hand. "Then stay put," he said coldly, "and listen."

For long tense moments they held a staring match. "Lady," Hank at last conceded on a note of resignation, "if I wanted to hurt you I would already have done it. Now why don't you just settle back and listen to what I have to say like a reasonably civilized woman? I've had a tough day and this isn't making it any better."

"I don't have a concussion," Gloria repeated, her tone as cold as his, but she relaxed slightly.

Again he stepped away from her, as if she were an unpredictable wild thing and he wanted to give her distance. His face, with its high cheekbones and dark eyes, held all the warmth of a stone dungeon.

Yet, for some reason, he seemed familiar to her.

From nowhere the image of a gray fuzzy kitten popped into her mind....

"You don't know that," the man said, returning her to the present with a vengeance.

"This pamphlet says all head wounds should be treated seriously," he continued. "And it says drowsiness is a bad sign."

"Look, Mr. Whoever-you-are, I was napping because I was tired. I, too, have had a tough day and I want to go home." Cancel that plaintive note, she thought disgustedly, and lifted her chin, hoping aggression would impair the man's hearing.

"Hank Mason."

An answer that totally confused her. Perhaps...

No way. She did not have time for, nor could she afford, a concussion.

"My name is Hank Mason," he clarified, "and the pamphlet says you should be observed for twenty-four hours."

Her flabbergasted expression was almost comical. She looked like a prim little girl sitting on his bed, with her knees together and her bare feet dangling. It wasn't until one looked at her wild wanton hair and her tiger's eyes that realization hit. This little girl was all woman.

Those golden eyes blazed at him now with enough heat to put the soothing, crackling fire to shame.

"I...do...*not*...have a concussion," she spat. "And if you think I'm going to stay here for twenty-four hours while you...you *look* at me, you've got another think coming, buster."

Hank couldn't think of anything he wanted less.

"Don't do it," he said warningly when she made to jump off his bed. "You're forgetting something."

"What?" Her tone was belligerent.

"Your husband," Hank replied nastily. "I left him a note and also notified your neighbor, as you requested. Melanie Hensley's going to tell your old man. When he gets here, I'll release you to his care."

The starch seemed to go out of her. "Oh."

She was such a feisty little thing that for a moment Hank wanted to laugh at her defeated stance, gather her into his arms and tell her everything was okay.

But Gloria wasn't down for long. Her back straightened and her face lit up. Gloria Pellman was a *very* bad liar.

"He works nights," she said, sweetly reasonable. "But he'll be off around midnight. If you don't mind taking me and Jamey home now, it will only be a couple of hours until my husband gets there. Then he can observe me." She frowned and added with cold dignity, "But I *don't* have a concussion."

Folding his arms across his broad chest and crossing his legs at the ankles—she noticed he wore moccasins instead of boots, though the rest of his garb was Western—Hank Mason's casual stance had all the give of a stone wall.

"You didn't say anything earlier about him working nights," he said. "In fact, you said he was waiting for you."

"I forgot."

He pounced. "Confusion. And when I woke you up, you didn't know where you were even though you were conscious when I brought you here earlier."

"My husband's on a new shift," Gloria said desperately. "It was natural to forget. And I didn't know where I was when you woke me because I was dreaming."

Glaring at him, she ordered, "Let me see that damn pamphlet."

When he handed it to her she muttered something about trying to practice medicine from a handout.

Gloria found she had to hold the paper right up to her face and squint.

"Blurred vision," Hank commented righteously.

"Bad lighting," she snapped. "The only light is that lamp halfway across the room." Before he could stop her she hopped off the bed and stomped to the lamp in question where she peered at the medical leaflet again.

"I'm not vomiting and I'm not nauseous," she pronounced, scanning the list of symptoms.

"But you haven't eaten anything," Hank reminded her. "Unless you ate while I was gone?" He raised an inquiring eyebrow.

"No," she said shortly and examined the list again. "I'm not dizzy. There's nothing wrong with my breathing. And—" enunciating precisely "—my speech is not slurred."

"It hasn't been twenty-four hours. All those things might happen later. That's why you need to be observed."

"Oh!" she said, so angry she couldn't find words to express her indignation. "Oh!" And she threw the brochure with all her might into the recliner beside the lamp.

The display of temper left Hank Mason unmoved. "Irrational behavior is also one of the symptoms," he remarked calmly.

"It is not."

Sighing, a small sound that further infuriated her, he walked to the kitchen area. "Look," he said. "Let's get this straight. I'm not taking you to a dark empty house tonight. And your neighbor can't stay with you because two in her family have the flu and she has all she can handle."

He took a couple of cans of soup from the cabinet and picked up a can opener. "You might as well resign yourself to staying put until your husband comes or I decide to take you home. Meantime—" he nodded toward the boy now sitting up and watching them silently "—do you suppose Jim is hungry? It's time to give your lack of nausea the supreme test."

Chapter Two

The fire had burned itself to coals.

Hank sat in the recliner, pushed back to its full extent. A towel draped the shade of the lamp beside him, limiting its glow to the immediate area.

Gloria Pellman lay in his bed, her son cuddled in her arms beside her. It was close to midnight. If her story was true, her husband should be here soon. But Hank wasn't holding his breath.

He glanced toward the far side of the room where the bed and the two people in it appeared only as a shadowed mass.

For which he was grateful. Something about the woman really got to him. She looked as if life hadn't treated her gently, yet she took on adversity with fire and fury and a sweetly outthrust chin...even when the adversity was nothing more than the shadows of her own imagination.

When he'd held her in his arms this afternoon in the trees he'd felt himself more than capable of slaying dragons.

Hank snorted softly. He might be attracted, but he wasn't stupid.

A few hundred years ago Gloria Pellman would have been burned at the stake. She was a witch, pure and simple—pure as mud and simple as quantum physics. There she was, skinny as a rail and, except for her tiger eyes, nothing much to look at. Yet the first time a man touches her, he's ready to protect her to the death.

But she'd met her match with him. He'd been the great male protector one time too many already.

Marina had appeared helpless, too. Small and blond, with large blue eyes that told a man how strong he was, she brought out the protective instincts in every male she met. Her soft feminine ways made him feel as if he were Lancelot, Sir Walter Raleigh, and Arnold Schwarzenegger rolled into one.

Again Hank's mouth quirked, a short derisive twitch.

He'd been such an easy mark.

Growing up with little or no family of his own, all his life he'd wanted the peace, comfort and stability of family living. In his early twenties he'd allowed the dream to become an obsession, working long hours to get his career in order, then looking around for a wife to complete the picture.

It was only after gut-wrenching self-analysis that he'd admitted the bitter disintegration of his dream had not been *all* Marina's fault.

Most of his experience before her had been with women who wanted the same empty party favours he wanted—a good time, a tumble, no strings. But when it came to the mother of his children, those girls weren't good enough. For that, he wanted a *nice* girl. Translate that to a combination Holy Virgin, Mary Sunshine, and Mrs. Partridge.

Enter Marina. Such a *nice* woman, whose gentle blue eyes covered a heart the size of a pea. She had wanted a home all right…one on Fifth Avenue, one in France, one in Vail and one in San Francisco. And her one pregnancy had been through a mix-up with her pills. It might possibly have been through a mix-up with her men, as well.

Hank gave another soft snort. Marina had certainly taught him a lot about being helpless.

So how could he have been so easily taken in by the woman now lying in his bed?

His attraction to her was something he didn't want, didn't need, and had no intention of pursuing, assuming she really was lying about the illusive husband. And Lord knew there were plenty of women in his life, women who could laugh the innocuous word *nice* right out of the dictionary.

It must have been the way Gloria Pellman's body felt, fitting so perfectly with his, that initially blew away his common sense, Hank decided. Well, he had it back now. This woman, with her nothing looks and her scrawny body and her black magic, was Trouble. And he planned to steer clear of her.

He closed his eyes and shifted a little, trying to get comfortable. It was going to be a long night.

When Jamey wriggled from her arms and flopped over onto his tummy, Gloria woke from a light doze. She, too, turned over so that his warm little body lay

at her back, and was settling into a quick return to
sleep when she realized a light shone in the darkened
room.

A light?

Recognition came almost immediately. The clean
smell that filled her nostrils—sunshine and meadow
grasses with an accent of woodsmoke—was the odor
of the sheets she lay on. They'd obviously been line-
dried outdoors. The woodsmoke odor came from the
fireplace where coals still glowed. The combined
smells were also the distinguishing odor of the man
in whose bed she now slept, the man whose cold
dismissing eyes angered her for some reason. He sat
in his chair, away from her and Jamey, alone in the
small pool of illumination cast by the lamp.

The Man, Gloria thought. Hank Mason. The man
she had hit.

Strange how she'd forgotten that part. Now she
remembered how in her first mindless uncompre-
hending fear, she'd hit him repeatedly. "I warn
you," he'd said at some point, but he hadn't hit her.
He'd hugged her instead, as if pulling her up next to
his heart gave her aggression no consequence.

The memory seemed totally ridiculous. That *was*
what happened, wasn't it?

Yes! she answered herself fiercely. You do not
have a concussion, Gloria Pellman. The man hugged
you. So what if for a second there the hug felt good?
Big deal.

Think strength, she further ordered herself, and
Hank Mason popped right back into her mind again.

Not his, you ninny! Your own!

She held her breath as the man shifted in his chair
and a fear she knew to be completely groundless

feathered up her backbone like the delicate paws of a fuzzy gray kitten.

Oh, for heaven's sake, Gloria thought angrily. Stop it! She wasn't afraid of the man. After all, he wasn't responsible for his craggy facial structure and lonely eyes with the onyx depth of marbles.

Lonely? Where had that thought come from?

The man was hard, hard as the mountains, and as uncaring. He was no Galahad, doing good deeds. Everything he'd done for her had been done reluctantly because there was no one else to do it. Hank Mason had just picked up a piece of flotsam off his mountain and had the misfortune not to have anything to do with it until morning. She didn't owe him a thing.

Gloria snuggled further into the warmth of the rough blanket and luxuriated in the feather pillow beneath her bruised head. The scent of masculine sunshine wafted through her senses. She slept almost at once.

Daylight filled the room.

Blinking her eyes in momentary bewilderment, Gloria heard birds arguing somewhere nearby, but no other sound. Levering herself onto one elbow, she looked around. Not only was it daylight, it was well into the morning. Good grief! She had things to do this morning, people to meet.

Swinging her legs over the side of the bed, she stilled. Jamey. Where was Jamey? Only to exhale a soft breath of relief. Her normally early rising son still lay curled into a little ball on the opposite side of the bed.

Gloria hopped off the bed, pulled on her jeans, and searched for her sandals. She needed to find the owner of the cabin, make her thank-yous, and get back to the ugly little house she and Jamey had left so hastily and lightheartedly the day before.

With one foot half into her sandal, she stopped abruptly. Shoes could wait. First and foremost, she needed a bathroom. It had been a very long time. How in the world had Jamey managed? He should be swimming by now.

The front door stood open to the freshness of the morning and that left only one other door in the cabin. Padding barefoot across the room, she opened the door and found herself peering into a clothes-cum-storage closet-cum-pantry.

"Looking for something?"

Rats!

Gritting her teeth at the appearance of being caught snooping, Gloria pasted a polite look on her face and turned slowly around.

"I was looking for the bathroom," she explained pleasantly to the man standing in the sun-filled doorway, and smiled. "This isn't it."

"Not last I looked," Hank Mason agreed, but he didn't smile, nor did he look especially put out. He merely looked knowing and cynical, as if she were doing exactly what he expected of her...snooping.

"If you want to wash your face," he continued, his face undergoing no change at all, "the sink there is used for washing everything. If you want a bath, the creek is right through the trees. But if you want the...uh...facility, it's the little house out back. There's no moon on the door."

"I'll try the uh-facility first," she replied, stealing some of his mockery without a qualm. She had started across the room to the open door when his low drawl stopped her.

"You might want your shoes. There's spiders."

Her back straightened perceptibly as she continued toward the door. "Spiders and I have an agreement. We leave each other alone."

Behind her, Hank bit back a reluctant grin, then brought himself up short. Trouble comes in just that sort of packaging, he reminded himself. And don't you forget it.

When she returned, Gloria found Jamey sitting on the side of the bed waiting for her. The man stood at the stove, frying bacon. Apparently, neither had made an attempt at conversation.

Jamey came forward to give her his morning hug and she ruffled his hair. "Good morning, honey. If you need the bathroom, it's around the back of the cabin."

Her son paused and looked from her to Hank then back to his mother.

"Mr. Mason doesn't mind if you use his bathroom, Jamey," Gloria said gently. "It's just not attached to the house."

When Jamey still looked reluctant, Hank explained. "I took the boy to a nearby tree last night when nature called. The real one is around back, Jim."

Jamey had actually let a strange man take him out into the dark? Amazing, Gloria thought. But she had another caution to make. "There's a big granddaddy of a gray spider in one corner of the bathroom, sweetie, but you don't need to worry. He's not the least interested in feet. In fact, he didn't seem to have much to say at all."

"His name's Charley," Hank said. "He never says much."

Jamey, afraid of most things human, was not the least bit afraid of other creatures, though Gloria had taught him not to touch any animal without both her permission and the animal's in question. Wide-eyed, Jamey hurried out the door eager to meet the silent Charley.

"There's coffee on the stove and mugs in the cabinet." Hank offhandedly tossed out his hospitality as Gloria slipped into her sandals—with her shoes on she felt more able to face the world with dignity. She then smoothed the sheets and blanket on the bed.

"And there's a comb in the top drawer of the chest if you want to use it."

She flushed. He'd said that on purpose, blast him. The man had a decided knack for making her feel at a disadvantage. First her shoes, now her hair.

"Thanks." But she darn sure wasn't giving him the satisfaction of watching her brush her hair after he'd treated her as if she was little older than Jamey and still needed to be told what to do. Defiantly, her hair remained wild about her shoulders as she crossed the room to pour herself a cup of coffee.

"Can you tell me how far we are from Tulaca, Mr. Mason?"

"About four miles. And next time you decide to go for a stroll in the country, dress properly. You fell because you were traipsing around the mountain dressed for a backyard barbecue. Shows no respect."

Gloria felt her temper rise at his dismissing words. She knew they were dressed inappropriately for hiking, but what was it to him? This cabin certainly wasn't the Houston Hilton.

"Someone must have pulled down the dress code sign," she replied tersely. "We'll know better next time."

Hank put the bacon on a plate covered with a paper towel, then began breaking eggs into the hot bacon grease, answering her barb without turning. "I meant, it shows no respect for the mountain. In sandals like those, you were bound to get hurt, but it wasn't the mountain's fault."

The small chastisement startled her. Hank Mason spoke of the mountain as if it were a living thing, a being with feelings, like Charley the spider. Yet there was no shadow of this fey sensitivity in his craggy face.

Without thinking, Gloria found herself explaining. "This mountain and all the range behind it fills the front windows of our house in Tulaca," she said slowly. "The windowsills frame it so that it's like a living painting, making even that ugly little room seem beautiful. When we arrived at the house yesterday Jamey and I just stood for a long time and stared through that window. My son had never seen a mountain and was fascinated. Before we even unpacked, we decided to explore a little. We started walking up the road and...and couldn't turn around again. There was always something more interesting to see further ahead."

She stopped abruptly, not about to tell this man that the clothing she and Jamey wore was all they had for daily wear. And although her sandals had made her legs ache, they were too worn and shaped to her feet to cause blisters.

The four-mile walk had been one of enchantment. Not until this morning did she realize how the walk had tired her—probably the reason she and Jamey had slept so late.

And then Gloria realized that nowhere in her narrative had she mentioned a husband.

But Hank wasn't thinking about Gloria Pellman's husband. She had just put into words the way he'd felt about this mountain for as long as he could remember. "A living painting," she called it. Exactly so. A painting that in the years of his growing up had been God, and hope, and defiance rolled into one.

Yet all he said now was, "There are plates in the cabinet and cutlery in the drawer to the left of the sink."

Gloria stiffened. Drat the man, he'd done it again, now making her feel a *lazy* snoop.

Pushing herself away from the countertop where she'd been leaning, sipping the hot delicious coffee, she placed her mug on the table with a decisive rap before turning toward the cabinet.

She was automatically setting the china and silver in their places, inwardly fuming, when suddenly her eyes widened. China and silver? Creamy, translucent china with a single silver ring around the edge. Lennox, she'd bet. And the heavy knives and forks she held in her hand bore the soft patina and old-fashioned pattern of antique sterling.

Last night they'd drunk their soup from Hank's old-fashioned restaurant-style coffee mugs and she'd been too tired to notice what kind of eating utensils they'd used.

"How beautiful," she whispered.

"I agree. Do you suppose the boy fell in?"

Hank Mason's drawl came like a splash of ice water, honey-flavored. Gloria stared at him, searching his chiseled face, trying to come to terms with a man who lived in a cabin with the austerity of a monk's cell, yet used fine china for breakfast dishes.

He stared right back at her, giving away nothing. Only his thick lashes indicated softness. She didn't trust them.

But she'd trusted them once, she thought.

Her mouth rounded to a soundless Oh! as she stared at Hank in astonishment. She knew who he was!

Now what? Hank thought, not sure he liked the look on Gloria Pellman's face. Her expression said she'd just identified him as the inventor of snooze alarms.

"Why, you're Hank," she exclaimed, a wide smile lighting her features.

His eyes narrowed warily. "That's right."

"I remember now," she explained in the face of his obvious puzzlement. "I know you."

"Look, maybe you better just sit down awhile."

He took her elbow before she had time to protest and began leading her toward the recliner.

Gloria promptly dug in her heels and jerked her arm from his grasp. "Don't you *dare* start that again. I know exactly what I'm saying. You rescued the kitten." She backed up hastily when he again reached for her, quickly adding, "A long time ago."

Hank didn't want her getting overexcited, so he folded his arms across his chest and made an effort to look casually interested. "Why don't you tell me about it?"

"Well, I don't really remember a whole lot. It was

years ago, after all, but you rescued my kitten. I was afraid of you."

"Mrs. Pellman. Glorie," Hank said coaxingly, "please sit down. You have me confused with someone else."

"Gloria," she corrected. "And I'm not confused. You were younger then, of course, but I remember your face very clearly."

"But I don't remember yours," he replied with dry reasonableness, not adding that if he'd ever met this woman before, he wouldn't have forgotten.

"Probably not. I was eight years old at the time," Gloria said, and he heard the rueful smile in her voice though her mouth remained grave.

"It was the year my parents and I spent the summer at the Redfern Inn in Tulaca," she continued. "Just before we left to return to Houston, Mr. Redfern gave me a kitten to take home. I don't remember how or why it went up the tree, but I remember crying because it wouldn't come down. You climbed up and got it for me."

"When I was a teenager, I sometimes worked for the Redferns," Hank acknowledged slowly, his face now a careful blank. He shook his head. "But I don't remember the incident."

Gloria twisted her mouth into a rueful grimace. "It was a long time ago. When I first saw you yesterday I thought you looked familiar in some way, but all I could remember until just a minute ago was a gray fuzzy kitten and fear. Actually, I'm surprised I even remember that much. We left for Houston that same day and I never came back to Tulaca...until yesterday."

Hank set the plates of fried eggs and bacon on the

table. "What brought you back?" he asked before he could stop himself. He already knew far more about this woman than he liked.

"A job. I'm computerizing the files at Mountain Country Realty and will be the office person when Mr. Hendryx is in the field. I wanted to see him this morning, but I suppose it will have to wait until tomorrow. It must be almost noon and I haven't even unpacked yet."

Hank sighed soundlessly. Wouldn't you know. Trouble seemed to follow Gloria Pellman like a second shadow. Should he give her the bad news now or let one of the Hendryx family tell her? Better wait. After all, it was none of his business.

Jamey came in at that moment, saving him from a reply.

"Wash your hands and face at the sink, Jamey," Gloria ordered briskly, glad to be centering attention on the mundane duties of child raising. For some reason, the kitten rescuing incident was beginning to make her nervous. She wished she hadn't brought it up. "What took you so long?"

"I was talking to Charley," her son answered gravely. Hank handed him a towel and he dried his face. "But he didn't talk back."

"Never does. Sit down, boy, and tuck in."

Hank's slow drawl had Jamey taking a seat at once and Gloria suddenly realized that while she had set three places, there were only two chairs. She looked around for the box Jamey had used the night before.

"I ate earlier, while you were sleeping," the lazy voice continued. "If you'll excuse me, I have chores to do outside."

It was a strange breakfast. Fine china and old sil-

ver on a rough handmade table with no cloth. Greasy
fried eggs, limp underdone bacon, burned toast and
delicious coffee in a thick plain earthenware mug.
Jamey drank his milk from a peanut butter glass with
cartoon characters printed on the outside.

The child followed Hank Mason's order and
tucked into his greasy breakfast with gusto. He ate
silently, accepting the strange hospitality with his
usual quiet stoicism. Gloria wondered if her son
would ever chatter like other small boys.

There was no sound in the cabin except the occasional clink of utensils and the incessant ringing
sound, coming from the outdoors, of an ax biting into
wood.

Gloria didn't eat much. Hank Mason might have
good intentions, but his cooking left much to be de-
sired. Instead she drank another cup of the fragrant
delicious coffee and let the peace, a hidden part of
the cabin's decor, work on her troubled spirit.

There was so much to do. She had to get back to
Tulaca and first thing in the morning pay a visit to
the real estate office. Her small savings was rapidly
diminishing and she needed to get started in her new
job as soon as possible.

Eric's life insurance checks should arrive some-
time soon, but she knew better than to rely on their
"coming" without a steady paycheck, as well. Bu-
reaucracy had a way of slowing the most straight-
forward issues to a crawl.

But she did have a job, she reminded herself. At
last, life was looking up. She was in Tulaca, home
of mountains and new beginnings. A small town with
minimal crime and the perfect place for a small shy
boy to grow.

And she had a house. So what if it was ugly? Mr. Hendryx had found it for her after telling her over the phone that housing was short in Tulaca because of the chemical plant under construction in the next town. He'd warned her the house was shabby, but Gloria had replied that it didn't matter. From her small savings account, she sent him the deposit and first month's rent, knowing she could be happy in a cave if Jamey was.

There were drawbacks to Tulaca being so small, but its very smallness meant she wouldn't need a car right away. With the public transit system in Houston she hadn't needed one, but to explore the wide-open spaces of her new home she would. However, there was no hurry. When the insurance money arrived she could get herself a car, one with four-wheel drive, perhaps.

The most pressing bit of business right now was to find someone to look after Jamey while she worked.

Gloria sighed. That was far from being as easy as it sounded. She touched the bruised spot on the back of her head absently. Her son *must* be happy here and learn to trust. He would start kindergarten in the fall and small children could be so cruel to those they thought weaker than themselves.

"May I go outside, Mama?" Jamey stood beside her chair, his serious little face turned up to hers. She felt a sudden anguished longing to hear him laugh. It had been too long.

"Run on, honey. Ask Mr. Mason if there's anything you can do to help," she added, doubting he would. Jamey didn't usually approach a man on his own. "As soon as I've finished with the dishes we're going back to town."

She didn't start the dishes right away, however. She brushed her hair, helping the brush by taming the strands with her hands and securing them with an elastic band at the nape of her neck. Then she replaced the soft T-shirt Hank had loaned her the night before with her sweater. The sweater chafed, making her long for a bath and a change of clothing.

When she went to wash dishes, Gloria found that a little more than usual was involved. For one thing, there was no hot water. The man had a decided knack for making simple things difficult, she thought resignedly, rummaging in the bottom of the cabinet to find a pan large enough to heat water in. And yes, I'm snooping, she told him silently, remembering his *Looking for something?* when he'd found her with his pantry door open.

But washing his china was a pleasure, and with the silver dried and shined back to its soft glowing beauty, she returned it to its drawer reverently. She, too, loved beautiful things.

Then she gave a little sigh and touched the bruised spot at the back of her head again. It still ached. Not badly, but enough to be uncomfortable.

"Do you want a couple of aspirins?"

"I...yes, please."

The man was disconcertingly cat-footed, standing beside her before she was even aware he was in the room. He held a bottle of painkillers in his hand and she opened her palm for him to shake the tablets into it.

Her eyes focused on his hand as he gave them to her. It was a beautiful hand, finely shaped with long, slim fingers. A hand that didn't go with a face of stone, she thought musingly. It was a hand that would be comfortable holding china and old silver or caressing a child's head.

"Are you all right?"

He held out a glass of water for her—a peanut butter glass with Bugs Bunny characters. Gloria fought back a giggle. Bugs Bunny didn't go with a fortress face, either. Nor, for that matter, did peanut butter.

"Yes, I'm fine, thank you. The bruise is just sore."

"You better have someone take you to the doctor when you get back to Tulaca. You aren't looking well."

She smiled at him coldly. "You do that on purpose, don't you?"

He only shook his head with apparent resignation and didn't answer.

Gloria didn't pursue it, merely walked out into the bright morning sunshine. Jamey sat on the step waiting for her. She turned and put out her hand.

"Thank you, Mr. Mason," she said with perfunctory politeness, "for your help and hospitality. You were very kind. Jamey and I will be on our way now, and leave you to your mountain."

He ignored the hand. "Get in the car."

"No, really," she protested. "You've done more than enough. It's a lovely morning and we can use the exercise. Even you must realize by now that I'm in no danger of concussion." It took as much effort as she could muster to keep the nastiness out of her voice. Hank Mason had only to lift an eyebrow, as he did now, to infuriate her.

Without answering he took her elbow and walked her to the passenger side of the Chevrolet.

She stiffened a moment, then capitulated, allowing him to guide her. The walk would be a long one and she had much to do this afternoon. And there was Jamey to consider. Her son wasn't used to mountain trekking. But by this time next year he would be, she thought to herself, and smiled a small satisfied smile.

The ride back to Tulaca was short. Hank flew on the straightaways, slowing only for the hairpin curves. The car rode silently, no clanks or rattles in spite of its age, the engine rumbling low like a contented cat. Only the trees flashing by on either side gave an indication of the speed at which they traveled.

When Hank pulled into the drive and stopped, Gloria sat with him in the car for a long moment, silently surveying the house. It was small, with no porch to soften its stark lines, only concrete steps leading to the peeling front door. The grass and a few spindly shrubs were uncut and uncared for, and the house as a whole badly needed fresh paint. It looked like what it was: a rental house, nobody's home.

Unconsciously, she straightened her shoulders. It was *her* home now, and in a few weeks it would look like it. She would see to that.

After opening the door to get out, Gloria rummaged in her purse for the key, only to have it taken from her hand when she found it.

"I'll check it before I leave. There have been many people living in this house over the years, mostly men on the construction crews once they started building the chemical plant outside Jakerville.

Is your husband one of the men brought in to work at the plant?''

''No.'' Oh, that sly, obnoxious man!

At the door Hank removed the note he'd written the night before and handed it to her without comment.

Gloria gritted her teeth.

Then he moved silently ahead of her into the house, prowling through the three rooms quickly. He wore his moccasins again, she noticed. They were one reason for his quietness, but his grace of movement also added to it. He didn't slam about as most men did, but opened and closed doors without undue noise.

Hank Mason was an extraordinarily silent man, Gloria thought. Yet she didn't find his silences uncomfortable.

What bothered her, what set her teeth on edge and made her want to scream at him, was the way he seemed to always put her on the defensive. Everything he said, but more important, what he didn't say, fairly shouted that he expected nothing of her but baseness.

Yet what difference did it make? He was nothing to her. His opinion shouldn't matter at all.

Finally Hank returned to the living room, his all-seeing eyes running over the cheap scarred furniture that came with the house, seeing the three equally scarred suitcases and small pile of taped cardboard boxes standing in the middle of the floor.

''Unless you want the company, you ought to have the locks changed. Several men probably still have a key to the house.''

Gloria's head snapped up and she walked to the

door to hold it open suggestively. ''Thank you *again,* Mr. Mason. So kind of you to bring us home,'' she gritted.

The cold black eyes swept 'round the shabby room once more and then roved over her with no change of expression. Gloria felt as shabby as the room.

''No trouble,'' the man said, leaving her with the distinct impression that had it been, she would still be on the mountain.

When he was gone and she heard the powerful motor of the car roar into life and then recede as he pulled away from the house, Gloria leaned against the closed door, shut her eyes, and released a pent-up sigh. When she opened them again she found Jamey sitting on the frayed and faded maroon couch watching her, his tawny eyes, so like her own, their usual serious study.

Forcing a smile, she straightened to order cheerfully, ''Bring your bag into the bedroom, honey, and I'll show you which drawers you can have for your things.''

Gloria put her own meager possessions away before making the bed with its surprisingly good mattress, using sheets she had brought with her. Linens came with the house, as did dishes and other household items, but she didn't like the thought of using sheets or towels that had been through someone else's uncertain washing.

As she smoothed her blue cotton spread over the bed and Jamey busily filled the two drawers she had given him with his few bits of clothing, a battered teddy bear propped against the chest watching with its one good eye, she heard a decisive knocking.

Frowning, Gloria walked through the living room to the front door.

Hank Mason stood there, a bulging brown paper bag held easily in one arm. When he thrust it toward her she took it automatically. Not speaking, he turned and walked back toward his car.

Glancing into the bag, Gloria found it full of groceries.

She flew down the steps after him to thrust the sack forward. "This isn't mine," she informed the man stiffly, her proud posture hampered by the heavy bag he didn't take back.

He looked down at her coldly. "It's part of the Welcoming Committee routine."

"No, thank you." Her voice held the same chill as his face. When she left Eric, she'd walked out with not even her purse and only the clothes she and Jamey had on their backs. She'd been forced to take charity throughout those hellish days, but had promised herself never ever to do it again. And she never had.

"Glen Bigelow at Bigelow's Mercantile supplied the stuff. If you don't want it, give it back to him."

Her stance didn't lessen its aggressiveness. "You're a bad liar," she told him thinly, and saw his mouth tighten.

He straightened, looking decidedly dangerous at her belligerence; a look that sent her heart knocking against her ribs like a prisoner's cup against cell bars. Perhaps she'd better drop the subject of lying.

Pride wouldn't allow her to completely back down, however. "All right. I accept, but only on condition that I pay for them. How much do I owe you?"

"Nineteen dollars and thirty-six cents." If her words were grudging, his entered the region on an Arctic cold front.

Turning on her heel, she marched back to the house. "If you'll step inside, I'll get your money," she said, her tone for all the world as if the man was a delivery boy.

He came right behind her, walking so softly that when she placed the bag of groceries on the kitchen table and turned to see what had become of him, her nose came close to colliding with his chest.

Menace hovered in the air of the small kitchen and Gloria dared not look into the face of the man looming over her. Though no part of him actually touched her, she felt trapped between the close proximity of his tall frame and the edge of the paint-chipped table.

Stepping to the side, she sidled past him, then hurried into the living room to take a twenty dollar bill from her purse, rummaging in the bottom of it until she had the thirty-six cents in exact change.

After handing him the money, she looked into the closed face at last. Hank Mason reached into the back pocket of his jeans to extract his wallet, placed the bill in it, and was in the act of taking out a one dollar bill when she said the unforgivable.

"Keep the change."

She swallowed. Oh, her pride! Her abominable, big-mouthed pride! She knew better. Knew the rudeness and crudeness of her words were an insult to any man west of the Mississippi River. The words hung in the air between them, quivering with spitefulness.

Hank eyed the woman's appalled features dispassionately. She had allowed her mouth to run away with her and she knew it, he thought. And what a delectable mouth it was. Gloria Pellman was going to apologize just as soon as she recovered her wits. Should he let her?

Nah.

He took her unresisting hand in his and folded the dollar bill into her limp palm, keeping a loose grip on the now closed hand. "*You* keep the change," he ordered softly. "I think I'd rather have another kind of tip." And he swooped to catch that runaway mouth of hers with his own. He also tightened his hold on her small fist—lifting just as he knew it would—and put his other arm around her shoulders to pull her closely against him, her free arm unable to do much damage.

She jerked once, but after that he didn't know what she did because the world jumped completely out of orbit before shrinking to the dimensions of his mouth on hers. What he'd meant as harmless retaliation, a mockery of touchdown and liftoff, backfired into a nuclear explosion.

For a moment Gloria stood acquiescent, unable to comprehend that she was being expertly kissed. She made a feeble effort to pull away from him, but Hank's arm around her shoulder was an iron band.

It didn't matter. She'd waited far too long to protest anyway, now caught fast in a sensual trap she'd never known was there. The mouth on hers mesmerized her, told her wonderful secrets about his body and hers, drank deeply from her lips and quenched her thirst at the same time.

More. She wanted more.

No! She wanted out. Out!

As if he read her mind, Hank Mason let her go. At least he looked as dazed and angry as she felt. She lifted her chin.

With confused eyes, Gloria watched him silently walk out the door.

Chapter Three

Hank let the Chevy ease up the mountain road at a sedate thirty miles an hour. Angry as he was, he knew better than to put a heavy foot to the accelerator. He was mad at Glorie Pellman for letting him kiss her. Most of all, he was furious with himself for doing it.

"Glori-a," he corrected himself cynically. That woman was nobody's glory. *Keep the change.* Ha!

Yet once he arrived at the cabin, he took two steps inside the place that had been his refuge for years, made an abrupt U-turn, and stalked right out again.

Glorie Pellman's ghost, plain as day and twice as insubstantial, stood in the kitchen area as if she owned it, a dish towel in one hand and the other holding up one of his plates. As she admired its beauty a soft smile curved the delicate lips he could still taste.

How had he known, Hank wondered angrily as his long strides took him through the trees, when he bought the damn dishes five years ago at an estate sale, that they would suit a warrior princess so exactly? At the time, they just seemed to suit him. Even so he'd laughed at himself as he loaded the box into the Studebaker he'd actually gone to the sale to buy.

From instinct, he headed to the cliff.

Standing at the cliff edge and determinedly gazing at the vista of mountains, ridge after ridge of them stretching to infinity, he conquered the Pellman woman's ghost easily.

But he couldn't conquer his own. His fifteen-year-old self stared at him with accusing eyes.

He'd lied through his teeth when he told Glorie that he didn't remember the kitten incident.

Sighing, Hank left the edge of the cliff and walked toward the nest of boulders where he'd often sat over the years. Perhaps he didn't actually remember Glorie, but the incident itself had changed him forever.

That long-ago summer he'd worked for the Redferns, tending the grounds around the old fifties-style "tourist court." The small happy family spending their vacation there had fascinated him. He timed his chores to watch a tall, slightly stoop-shouldered father swing his daughter on the old tire swing in the playground, and listened to the child laugh in delight, demanding, "Higher, Daddy! Higher!"

He watched father, mother, and child walk over the grounds to their car, hand in hand with the child in the middle, the three of them leaving to visit tourist sights in the area or for a drive through the mountains.

One time he saw the dark-haired mother laugh-ingly grab her daughter under the arms and whirl her 'round and 'round and 'round till both were breathless.

Even then Hank knew and accepted that God had fashioned his face with hammer and chisel rather than using His usual soft clay and deft, loving hands. The child was afraid of him. When Hank was in the vicinity, she hid behind her father's pant leg and stared at him unsmilingly. If he appeared when she was alone, she scurried back to her family's room.

Her fear didn't bother him. The teenage girls, beginning to look over his tall gangly person with appreciative eyes, thought he looked just fine. More important, the child's mother and father spoke to him in a friendly fashion whenever they passed him doing his outdoor work.

Then there was the incident with the kitten.

Early one morning he came around the corner of one of the units to find the child standing beside the tire swing, sobbing loudly with a mixture of anger, fear, and distress. Apparently her family didn't hear the wails because no one responded.

"What's wrong?" Hank had asked.

For once, the little girl's fear of him was forgotten. "He scratched me," she said in tearful indignation. "Then he ran up the tree and now he won't come down."

"He" was obviously the gray kitten Mr. Redfern had given her from his mama cat's most recent litter. Hank looked up, and sure enough, the little cat sat placidly on a low branch of the old tree dominating the playground. It was out of the child's reach but not out of his. In moments it sat just as placidly in the palm of a large hand the rest of his teenage body was still trying to match.

The child's tears stopped like magic but when she went to reach for her pet, Hank held it protectively. "Wait," he'd said, and remembered even now the storm clouds that immediately began to gather in the small piquant face, though he didn't remember the face at all.

"Do you see how I'm holding him?" he asked. Still cradling the kitten, he squatted in front of her before the child could express the tirade about to burst from her highly indignant person. "Kittens like to think they can do anything they choose," he explained quickly. "So you have to hold them gently. Usually, when they know they can leave, they stay put just to be contrary."

She'd giggled at that, Hank remembered, but he didn't remember the giggle—just the fact. He had smiled back at her.

Then she'd done what he recalled now as if it were yesterday.

Glorie Pellman, or whatever her last name was all those years ago, had put her thin scratched arms around his neck and hugged him...hard. Probably as exuberantly and hard as she'd hugged the kitten so that it scratched her and ran.

Hank didn't scratch and he didn't run. He squatted there in the sunny playground of the Redfern Inn with the same stillness as the boulders on the mountain, cradling a gray tabby kitten in his palm and locked in a child's impetuous embrace.

Odd that he had no recollection of Glorie's unusual golden eyes or the dark waywardness of her hair, but he could remember vividly the strength of her thin coltish arms, the warm tear-damp feel of her face against his cheek and the healthy, sweaty, sun-shiny odor of her small person.

He thought he remembered her taking the kitten and going back to her parents' room where they were packing to leave, but he couldn't be sure. That part was hazy, as was whatever excuse he made to Red-fern for leaving early.

Pursued by an emotion he couldn't identify—then or now—he'd fled to the mountain, to this very spot.

It had taken a child's strong arms to burst his own childish bubble. For he realized then just what it was he'd been trading for over the years with his small acts of kindness. *Love me,* he'd been saying. *I'm a good boy, just like a son.*

The knowledge of his hidden ulterior motive had left him weak, empty, and ashamed. That day he'd formed his empty dream. Someday he.*would* have a family, but it wouldn't be someone else's. It would be one of his own creation.

He'd gone back into Tulaca and left behind forever the needy teenager whose lost soul still wandered among the rocks.

No one in town knew there was a difference in the boy Hank Mason, but Hank knew. He never mowed old Mrs. Schaffer's lawn again, or fixed Gus Lucas's truck, that he wasn't aware of exactly what he was doing. He couldn't stop, of course—too many people depended on his strong young back. But it was enough that now he understood himself and could guard against his own weakness.

None of those people ever gave him the uncon-ditional hug the child Glorie had, although they pat-ted him on the back approvingly, invited him to

Thanksgiving dinner, and had a box for him at Christmas filled with something homemade. But he recognized the trade-off for what it was....

One lone star hung low in the deepening twilight sky when Hank finally left the cliff and returned to the cabin. He had it to himself again. Except for the faintest feminine scent in his feather pillow, Glorie Pellman was gone.

Knocking on the peeling front door, Hank heard the trace of belligerent impatience echoing in the sharp staccato. He was crazy to be here. Two days ago the woman had treated him like dirt and insulted him.

Taking off his Stetson, he ran a hand through his hair before knocking again.

He'd been to Boulder to deliver the Chevy, then on to Santa Fe to pick up a Mustang. It was an unnecessarily hurried trip that had left little time for sleeping or eating over the past two days. Now he felt wrung out and pegged on the line to dry, not to mention he had a pounding headache beating into the back of his eyes like a giant hammer. The combination left his temper honed to a fine edge. After driving all night, what possible reason could he have for standing on these wobbling cement steps first thing in the morning? Hell, he hadn't even been to the cabin yet.

He was mad at himself because he hadn't told Gloria Pellman about Hendryx. Had she talked to the family yet? Was she all right?

And why should he care? *Nice* women could always take care of themselves. The majority of men loved nothing better than rescuing damsels in distress.

As he was about to turn away, the door opened with a small protesting *screek.* Just a slit, forcing Hank's eyes to follow its narrow trail downward until halted by a one-eyed, unwinking, golden brown stare coming at him from about hip level.

Hank made a conscious effort to ease the frown from his face. "Hello, kid. How're you doing?"

No answer, but a peanut butter-smeared face gradually revealed itself as the door swung open farther. The boy stood silently gazing up at him, looking small and neglected in his too small T-shirt decorated with liberal amounts of peanut butter and jelly down its faded front. His white-blond hair flopped in tufts over his forehead.

Hank clearly heard his grandmother's cracked strident voice floating waspishly down through a couple of dozen years, *It's one thing to be poor, but there's no excuse for dirt.* Perhaps Gloria Pellman wasn't so nice after all.

Disgust threatened to swamp him and he forced a deep controlling breath into his lungs so he could speak without snarling. "Where's your mother, Jim?"

The softly spoken answer clinched it. "In the bedroom."

Hank's nostrils flared. "And your dad?"

"I don't know. He...he doesn't l-live here."

Without a word Hank pushed open the door and stepped into the living room, the toe of his boot knocking aside one of Jim's blocks. Through the open kitchen door he saw dirty dishes on the table, a cereal box and milk carton evidence the boy had probably prepared his own breakfast.

"Get your mother, boy," he ordered tersely.

Jamey had taken a seat at the end of the hideous purple couch, his eyes seeming to fill his face. He trembled visibly.

"I'm not supposed to bother her now," he whispered. "She's…she's doing things in there and she…she's talking."

Talking, huh? In the bedroom and separated from her husband. Hank's lip curled. Her kind were all too common. Why did they have to have kids?

"All right, Jim. I'll get her for you. Go to the kitchen and wash your face, then change your shirt." He strode purposefully toward the bedroom. The door was open. If she didn't bother about privacy, why should he?

"I don't know how to get my shirt over my head."

Hank stopped and turned back with a frown. The child seemed to push himself further into the cushions of the couch. "Guess that could be a problem," he said easily. "I'm not going to do it for you, but I'll show you the trick to it."

He squatted to the level of the trembling child, but aware of Jamey's fright, carefully avoided touching him.

"Cross your arms in front of you, like so, and take the bottom of your shirt in your two hands. Now, raise your arms and let them gradually uncross themselves, holding on to the shirt. That's it. Now get yourself a clean one and wash your face."

Straightening, he turned away. The boy didn't actually smile, but his eyes shone like bronze coins at his small accomplishment. Skinny little runt, Hank thought. His mother ought to be horsewhipped.

Gloria Pellman wasn't in the bedroom and neither was anyone else.

But he could hear her talking, as the boy had said...a running litany of euphemisms that was as close to cursing as a woman could get who had a young son within earshot. Suddenly Hank grinned.

Wet towels lay strewn over the bedroom floor and he waded through a thin layer of water, heading for the partially opened bathroom door.

The mutter of "pipes" and "*Mayflower,*" a couple of varicolored "damns" and a not quite suppressed "Hell!" led him on. Then, "Jamey! Bring me a knife, would you please? Not a sharp one. One with a round end." A pause, then a mumbled, "Dammit! If I could just get this blasted doohickey..."

"Planning on cutting someone's throat, Ms. Pellman?" Hank asked mildly, pushing the door the rest of the way open and surveying the woman hunched halfway under the bathroom sink.

"No. But I don't have a screwdriver. If I take this handle off, I think I can put it back on again good enough to turn the water all the way off. I've got it from a gusher to a running drip but the damn thing just won't *stop* dripping," Gloria said, as if having Hank Mason standing in the middle of her flooded bathroom was the most natural thing in the world.

Then she looked up sharply. "What are you doing here?"

To his surprise, Hank answered with the literal truth. "Came to see how you were getting along."

Gloria frowned, too wrapped up in her flooded

bathroom to be offended. "As you see, I'm doing swimmingly."

Jamey appeared in the doorway with the kitchen knife she'd requested. "Thanks, honey," she said and swung back under the old-fashioned sink to try to unscrew the handle of the cutoff valve.

"I don't want to meddle in your business, Ms. Pellman," Hank said slowly, "but I wouldn't do that if I were you."

Instantly, as he'd known would happen, Gloria ducked back out to fix him with a cold glare. Then she sighed. "Meddle in my business, *please*. I haven't the foggiest idea what I'm doing."

He squatted on his hunkers and looked at the dripping pipe. "Well, if you take off that handle, you're not going to have a drip anymore," he drawled. From the corner of his eye he saw Glorie's face brighten in self-congratulation only to drop ludicrously when he added, "You're going to have Niagara Falls."

"You're doing it again," she accused, but without any real bite.

"You jump so quickly to conclusions, it's hard to resist," Hank murmured before adding, "It would be better to turn the water off outside at the main valve."

Gloria was still hunched half under the sink beside him and he saw her shoulders droop. With strands of her hair pulled out of its elastic band and her forest green T-shirt spotted liberally with damp, he had to fight the urge to kiss her.

"I tried that," she said. "But if there's a cutoff valve in the yard someplace, I couldn't find it. I also went next door to call the plumber. Tulaca only has one, but he has the flu.''

Hank stood, glad for an excuse to get off the bathroom floor and out of such close quarters with this witch woman. ''You have to know where to look,'' he said, and added, ''For the cutoff valve, not the plumber. You're right. There's only one.'' And he left the room, heading for the backyard and telling himself it wasn't *really* full retreat.

When he returned, Gloria was bent over the bathtub trying to wring out large sopping towels. The pipe had stopped dripping. He put the wrench he'd borrowed from the Hensleys on the covered commode seat and knelt beside her to reach for a towel. His larger hands could make easier work of it than Gloria Pellman's.

''No,'' she said sharply. ''This I can do. But, um, thanks anyway. And...um...I didn't tell you, but th-thanks for the groceries, too. It was a...a thoughtful thing to do. I mean it,'' she added, but kept her face averted and squeezed on a wet towel for all she was worth.

Hank didn't comment but left her to her towel wringing. Yes, she meant it, he thought, biting back another of those reluctant grins she seemed to call up in him so easily. And it was killing her. He picked up the borrowed wrench and within seconds had a length of pipe in his hand.

''Here's your problem.''

Gloria looked at the pipe. Except for a couple of inoffensive rust spots, it looked fine to her. ''It is?''

''It is.'' Hank stood. ''I'm going to the hardware store. I'll be back in a few minutes.''

The towel in Gloria's hand landed back in the

bathtub. "Wait! I mean…just a minute. I'll get some money for you." She felt heat climb up her neck and into her cheeks. Her chin went up.

Black eyes gleaming suspiciously, Hank Mason's expression didn't change. "All right," he agreed, only to add blandly, "I don't know how much it will be. Seems like it might be more—" briefly, he searched for the word "—uh, *efficient* for me to buy what I need, bring back the receipt, and you—" lifting an eyebrow "—reimburse me?"

He waited, pretending not to notice Glorie's face was a wash of color. He thought her chin couldn't get any higher. He was wrong.

"Perhaps you're right," she said stiffly, and visibly swallowed. "Thank you."

As Hank pulled out of the weed-choked driveway he chuckled, then laughed outright. He was still smiling as he browsed the pipefitting aisle, but the smile died a quick death when he saw Jake Paulson, the owner of the hardware store, watching him speculatively.

"Problems at the cabin?" Jake asked as he took Hank's money.

"No." And that's all he's damn well getting from me, Hank thought as he picked up his sack and left. Which is not to say Jake wouldn't know before the day was over exactly whose plumbing problems Hank was fixing.

Tulaca was like that.

Gloria had just emerged from the bathroom, mop in hand, when Hank returned. His closed face made her pause momentarily before she mentally shrugged. Whatever the man's problem was, she certainly hadn't *asked* him to fix her leaking pipe. If he was sorry now for volunteering, too bad.

"Your receipt is on the table," he said coldly, and closed himself in the bathroom.

Opening the door again fifteen minutes later he found Gloria in the bedroom tucking her son into the double bed.

"Tummy ache," she explained briefly. "While I stemmed the tide, Jamey had a field day with the peanut butter and jelly. That was on top of what looks like most of the cereal."

She smiled down at Jamey comfortingly, brushed the flop of hair off his forehead, and said without looking in Hank's direction, "He doesn't yet understand moderation."

The words were chiding, but Hank heard the smile and the love in her voice.

He walked to the bed and examined the small figure huddled there. The boy's hair was only a shade darker than the white pillow slip. "Sorry about this, Jim," he said in genuine commiseration. He didn't feel so hot himself.

The boy nodded in solemn agreement.

"Lord, what a morning and it's not even ten o'clock yet," Gloria said tiredly, joining Hank a few minutes later in the kitchen where he stood, looking out the back door with his hands thrust in his back pockets.

He turned to see her pull the elastic band from her hair, smooth the wild mass with her palms, and use the elastic to tame it back into submission.

"You should wear it loose," he said, immediately wishing he hadn't.

For no reason at all, Gloria's heart rocked and she

tasted again that wild unexpected kiss of two days ago. Without looking at him, she turned on the tap and began filling the coffeepot before answering lightly, "Not a chance. It's so thick, when I wear it down I look like a witch." *Which is probably what you think I am,* she added silently.

Which is exactly what you are, Hank thought silently. *Why else would he be standing in this godawful kitchen exchanging polite chitchat?*

"Would you like a cup of coffee?"

Hell, why not? He'd fixed her sink, hadn't he? "There's a package of doughnuts in the car. I picked them up at a place in Santa Fe this morning," he said. "You do the caffeine. I'll do the cholesterol."

Real cosy, Mason, Hank told himself bitterly, reentering the dingy little house with the white pastry sack in his hand. *You damn fool.*

His first bite of glazed doughnut, on top of his already queasy stomach, confirmed that opinion. And after taking a sip of Gloria Pellman's coffee, if she could call it that, he knew he was in trouble.

Gloria sighed audibly as she watched Hank's face pucker. "It's all right," she said. "Don't be polite. I am a good cook, you know. But for some reason I don't make good coffee." *Although I don't think it's* that *bad,* she thought as Hank's dark face went a pasty tan. *Still, Hank had made her a cup of coffee to die for.*

Hank focused on Glorie's face to avoid the dark quivering surface of the evil stuff in the cup before him. "Guess we all have our talents," he said. "Me, I make good coffee, but I can't cook worth a damn."

He switched the subject off food completely. "Have you been to the real estate office yet?"

"No. I called there three times yesterday to let Mr. Hendryx know I arrived and to set up a time for meeting with him, but no one ever answered. I was going to try again this morning but I haven't had time to hoof it down to the corner to use the pay phone. With their family sick, I hate to keep borrowing my neighbor's phone." She smiled. "When Jamey wakes up I'll walk back to the corner."

Hank groaned silently. Dammit. She still didn't know.

"Glorie." He took a deep breath. "Uh, Ms. Pellman. Graydon Hendryx died of a heart attack several days ago. He was buried the day you arrived."

Gloria sat perfectly still, unable for several seconds to breathe. "No. Oh, no. That can't be. Someone would have notified me," and only realized she spoke aloud when Hank answered her.

"It's true," he said. To avoid taking her suddenly trembling hands in his own, he left the table to get the coffeepot and top off Gloria's coffee. "I don't know why you weren't advised," he added, taking his place at the table again and noticing that her hands were now in her lap.

"Perhaps one of Hendryx's sons is going to take over the office and wants to carry on the old man's plans." Hank kept his voice carefully neutral and now felt a twinge of guilt at the sudden fusion of hope that leapt into the woman's face. He found, however, that he could face that look much better than he could tolerate the abject despair that for brief seconds had looked out of her golden eyes.

Her shoulders straightened and she picked up her coffee cup with a hand as steady as a heart surgeon's. "Then when Jamey wakes up, I'll call the Hendryx home,'' she said, her voice as steady as her hand, ''and find out.'' Her chin was right out there where he knew it would be.

Without thinking, Hank took a swallow of coffee. He regretted it.

''If you want to call now,'' he said to get his mind off the tidal wave his thoughtless swallow set up in his stomach, ''I'll stay with the boy.'' He regretted the words immediately, too. What he wanted was to get out of here. The house always had that effect on him.

''Jamey will be frightened if he wakes and I'm gone,'' Gloria said slowly, and Hank breathed a sigh of relief that ended when she continued. ''But he's sound asleep. I doubt he wakes up for another hour.''

She stood. ''I shouldn't be more than fifteen minutes.''

Okay, Hank thought in resignation as Gloria returned to the bedroom for a last check on her son. I can handle fifteen minutes.

I hope.

When she returned to the kitchen she had changed her jeans and T-shirt and was carrying a nearly empty bottle of pink medicine in her hand.

''I'm almost out,'' she said. ''And Jamey feels a little warm. The drugstore is just a block past the phone.'' She was already heading for the door. ''I'll be right back. Twenty minutes, tops.''

An hour and ten minutes later she returned.

The first thing Gloria saw when she entered the living room was an unzipped sports bag on the floor near the end of the couch. The kitchen, where she'd left Hank sitting at the table, was empty, the small house itself eerily quiet.

Her heart dropped. *Jamey!* Five running steps and she was through the bedroom door, only to halt abruptly.

Jamey was sound asleep, curled in his usual tight little ball, but tucked up against Hank Mason's broad chest and encircled protectively by one lean-muscled arm. The man's black fathomless eyes watched her without expression.

Her eyes swung incredulously back to Jamey as she realized he had been put into one of Hank's T-shirts, making him look like Popeye's Swee'Pea.

What was going on here? Before she could give voice to the confused anger rising in her, Hank's soft drawl floated into the stillness of the shabby room.

"Not now. If you wake the boy, I'm not going to be happy. He's been a mighty sick youngster and needs his rest."

Her gaze dropped to her son's pale features and she saw the tracery of blue veins through the skin at his temples. His mouth was bloodless and the white-blond hair looked dull and lifeless. Clutched under his chin was his ragged, much loved Teddy. Clutched in his other hand was Hank Mason's thumb.

But there was little tenderness in the hard face above her son's sleeping one. Hank's black eyes were empty of expression...and yet the big man pulled his thumb from the child's grip with infinite care and, barely disturbing the bed, rolled away from the small body. He passed Gloria without so much as a nod and headed toward the bathroom.

In spite of Hank's warning, Gloria roused Jamey enough for him to swallow some of the medicine she brought, but he went right back to sleep. From the corner of her eye she saw Hank pass behind her as she straightened the sheets.

"I'm sorry I took so long," she said when she returned to the living room to find him zipping the sports bag. "The drugstore was a madhouse. I knew as soon as I overheard the symptoms everyone was discussing that Jamey must have come down with it. The pharmacist recommended I call the doctor for a prescription and then I had to wait my turn to have it filled."

"No problem," Hank said briefly.

"May I give you lunch before you go?" she asked. "It's not much by way of payment after your kindness, but..."

"No thanks," he interrupted, looking as if sitting down to a meal with her sickened him. "I'm leaving now." He glanced around for his Stetson.

Gloria, still smarting from his dismissing words, spotted it hanging on an unlikely nail on the far wall and went to get it for him. When she turned back with it in her hand she suddenly put the hat behind her back. "Mr. Mason, you look awful."

There was little left in Hank now but grim determination. "Getting your own back, are you?" he asked nastily. "I'm just feeling a little queasy, that's all. Probably from your coffee." Though her coffee should be long gone. There for a while, he and Jim had hung their heads over the commode together.

"It's more probably the stomach flu," Gloria answered, a hint of unrepentant merriment lurking in her eyes.

He scowled at her. "I'm never sick. Now if you'll excuse me..." He plucked his hat from her hand before she quite knew what he was about, picked up the sports bag he'd brought in to give Jim a clean shirt, and headed for the front door—only to find Glorie standing squarely in front of it.

He gave her his best glare. "You're not funny."

"You are." Her smile broadened to a malicious grin as he stiffened. "I advise you not to argue. It only makes the headache worse." She studied his face with interest. "You're an interesting shade of green, you know."

For answer, Hank put down his bag, lifted her easily to the side, then picked up the bag again and opened the door.

"If you walk out of here, Mr. Mason, I'll follow you and throw the biggest screaming fit this town has ever seen." Her voice was quiet, now totally devoid of humor.

Hank Mason turned to her from where he stood on the top step of the porch, a genuine smile touching his mouth and lighting his eyes, causing her to catch her breath.

"You'll do it, too, won't you, little Glorie? Lord, you're a cussed woman. Well, you better take a deep breath because…"

His smile slid into oblivion. "Oh, God." With stiff dignity, he walked back into the living room, through the bedroom, and beelined for the bathroom.

When he emerged, Gloria was waiting for him with Jamey's medicine in her hand. It was all she had for the moment and she poured him a double dose.

Popping the spoon into his mouth before he could object, she ordered with quiet authority, "Now get to bed."

"Are you propositioning me?" he asked snidely,

but Gloria could tell the man wasn't anywhere near top battle form.

"Green isn't my favorite color," she replied with no offense, and turned him toward the bed where Jamey lay sleeping.

By now, Hank had lost all desire to argue.

He sat on the edge of the bed and, with Gloria's help, pulled off his boots. Using her as a lever, he hauled himself upright again, where in one smooth and totally unexpected motion, he shucked his pants, revealing a very *brief* pair of continental black silk briefs.

"Can't stand sleeping in my clothes," he muttered with no regard at all for Gloria, who stood in shocked silence at his side. He dropped onto the bed with a sigh, his face like parchment under his tan.

The bouncing of the bed woke Jamey, who sat up groggily. "Sorry, Jim. Go back to sleep now," Hank said with his eyes closed against his headache and nausea.

Gloria pulled the sheet over him as Jamey lay down and promptly went back to sleep.

"The kid ought to argue more," Hank muttered, and was vaguely surprised when Jim's mother answered.

"He has his moments. Like you, he's biddable because he's ill. If you'll sit up a second and take this medication I'll leave you alone and you can go back to sleep, yourself."

Hank felt a cool hand against his throbbing forehead and struggled to open his eyes. Glorie sat on the side of the bed, her hair in two braids crowning her small head. When had she done that? he wondered vaguely. Tawny brown eyes trapped his attention.

"You have smiling eyes," he said, or thought he said, because the words seemed to float around the room. "God, my head hurts." He tasted the bitter taste of something syrupy, then felt his head back on the pillow with no idea how it got there. It pounded and his stomach was gripped in a giant crushing fist.

"I think I'm dying."

"No, you're not. Just a virulent case of the same stomach bug everyone else in town has. The doctor was here to make sure you stay in the land of the living." A gentle smile floated in the voice above him.

"But my eyes won't open."

"You're just too tired to open them. Go back to sleep. It's dark now, anyway."

"You have an answer for everything." Even to himself he sounded like a petulant little boy. God! Struggling, he sat up and forced his eyes open.

The bed depressed beside him at once and he saw her darkened outline in the dimness of the room. "Glorie?"

"What is it, Hank?"

"How's Jim?"

"Up and playing yesterday and today. Asleep beside you now. Are you feeling better?"

"Yes." His voice held an element of surprise. He lay back and closed his eyes once more. "You have to be tired, also. Why don't you lie down and get some sleep?"

Again came that golden smile in her voice. He seemed to have been listening to that smile forever.

"I've been resting on the other side of Jamey. It's three o'clock in the morning."

"Will you lie beside me?"

He felt her instant withdrawal even through his tiredness and groped for her hand before she could leave the side of the bed. "I meant nothing by it, Glorie. Just lonely, I suppose."

The admission shocked him. He hadn't acknowledged loneliness since he was fifteen. To change the subject, he asked, "How long have I been here?"

Gloria relaxed, but only slightly. For some reason she feared Hank Mason when he was civil, yet had no trouble at all handling him when he was his usual self and just short of insulting. She tried to remove her hand but he held it fast.

With an effort, she kept her voice even, betraying nothing of her madly racing pulses. "You've been sick three days and three nights. The doctor came last night because you weren't responding to the medication. He gave you an injection and then another one this morning. If a bed had been available, you would be in the hospital now."

The grasp on her hand tightened and there was a long silence. "I hate hospitals," he said at last.

There was something in his voice, in the tension of his hand as it held hers.

"Why?" she asked gently.

Again there was a long silence and she thought he was not going to answer.

"My sister and I were in the hospital with neglected cases of German measles. Anna lay in the bed next to mine in the children's ward. We were both pretty sick, but Anna was...." He stopped, then slowly continued.

"In the night she called to me. She was scared, she said, so I left my bed and crawled into hers while the nurse wasn't looking. While I told her a story, Anna kind of drifted into sleep. After a while I dozed off, too, still holding her hand. I never knew quite when she...just wasn't there anymore."

Gloria gripped tightly the long slim fingers linked with hers. "How old were you?" she asked softly, and closed her eyes in the numbing pain of his bald answer.

"Seven."

She couldn't speak, couldn't make her voice work around the tightness in her throat, but Hank's voice continued in the darkness as if the words were pulled from him without his consent.

"The next time I had reason to go to a hospital, my wife had miscarried our baby daughter."

The fingers were biting into hers now but Gloria barely registered the pain. "You're married?"

An ugly chuckle slid into the soft darkness of the quiet room. "Not for years. And Marina claimed it was better that we lost the child." He paused a moment before adding on a faint note of resignation, "She was right, I suppose. Ours was a marriage made in hell. By the time Marina got pregnant there was little love on either side."

But pain for the lost baby spread acid rivulets through his molasses drawl. Without thought, Gloria leaned down and rested her head on his shoulder, feeling his arms come up to cradle her gently, the fingers she had held now threaded through the mass of her hair. One of her hands cupped his cheek as she lay without speaking, offering him the only comfort she could give.

A soft sigh whispered above her head before he said with a touch of his old mockery, "Three in the morning. The hour when man confronts his life and invariably comes out the loser. I read that somewhere."

Gloria turned her face into his neck and touched his mouth with her fingers. "Hush," she whispered. "Go to sleep now."

He didn't answer, but rubbed his fingers over her skull, gently, rhythmically, until the movement stilled and grew weighted.

In her awkward position half on top of him, Gloria listened as Hank's breathing slowed and deepened. The hypnotic beat of his pulse throbbed above her temple.

When the arms around her at last grew slack, she pulled away from him to crawl in on the other side of the bed. She was tired herself, having had only short periods of rest the last few days, and was soon deeply asleep, unaware when Hank rose on one elbow, reached across her son's sleeping form between them, and drew the sheet more closely around her shoulders. Then he, too, lay back and returned to sleep.

Gloria awoke to find Jamey standing by the bed looking down at her. "I'm hungry, Mama."

She reached out and gave him a one-armed hug, noting with satisfaction that the unhealthy pallor of his recent illness had completely gone. "Me, too. What will it be this morning? Scrambled eggs or scrambled eggs?" She spoke softly so as not to wake the sleeping man beside her.

Jamey closed his eyes, pretending to give her

question serious thought, an adept player in this familiar game. "I'll have...scrambled eggs," he announced.

"Scrambled eggs it is. Scoot now. I'll be there in a minute."

She lay watching as her son left the room, clad in his too small X-Men pajamas. He flashed her a grin at the door and she smiled back, the smile vanishing as he disappeared.

Now, she thought grimly, to get myself out of this mess.

Hank Mason lay in the space previously occupied by Jamey, probably finding more comfort in the added room the boy's absence had given him. There was no telling how long her son, an early riser, had been up, but Hank had certainly made himself comfortable. He lay on his side, half on Gloria's nightgown, his bare legs tangled with hers, one lean-muscled arm pulling her back up against his broad torso in the same protective way he had held Jamey.

All well and good, but Gloria Pellman didn't need to be protected by the Hank Masons of this world.

Still, just for a moment she allowed herself to rest against him, an occasional little rumble attesting to his deep sleep. She found the soft intermittent snores an oddly comforting sound. It had been four years since she'd shared a bed with a man. If a week ago someone had predicted this morning's scene to her she would have laughed in their face.

The undersides of her breasts tingled against the arm just beneath them. For a moment she imagined their weight cupped in brown calloused hands.

At the thought, her breath shallowed and she became aware of the hard pelvic muscles cradling her hips, the masculinity pressing below them, and the muscled thighs bracing her legs. Her body felt charged, cell to cell with the body behind it. The body of Hank Mason, who slept on, unaware that from the first time he had touched her on the mountain, he became the enemy...for no other reason than being the only man in four long, horrible years to make her feel like a woman.

Gloria moved restlessly and the arm tightened under her breasts as the rhythm of Hank's breathing altered, only to deepen again when she stilled. His warm breath stirred her hair. For a moment she imagined turning within his oblivious embrace to...to be alive again, to be whole again.

Her body throbbed, begging for fulfillment. A cracked corner of her heart wept without tears.

The moment she put Hank Mason into her bed she'd known it to be a foolish move. Yet there'd really been no choice. Hadn't Hank cared for her and Jamey on the mountain? And this was the only bed in the house. The couch was only just longer than a love seat and much too short for herself or Hank, especially as sick as he'd been. Only Jamey fit on it, and Jamey was afraid to sleep by himself. Besides, his small presence had been needed in the bed.

Look what happened when he wasn't in it.

Gloria's eyes flew open as realization hit. What in heaven did she think she was doing?

Angrily she sat up, untangling her legs and tugging her gown from under the prone body beside her without regard to waking him.

But the man merely turned over onto his back, throwing the arm that had been around her over his head, his breathing no less deep and peaceful.

She scowled down at him, noticing the play of muscles over his hairless sculptured chest, the rise and fall of his flat taut abdomen where the sheet stopped just below his navel.

Just for a second, her stomach flip-flopped before she snatched up her bathrobe and hurried from the room.

Chapter Four

Gloria and Jamey were eating breakfast when she heard the shower. Where had Hank found the stamina, she wondered, to be up already? He had been more ill than most, according to the doctor, who had also commented that it often happened that way when exceptionally healthy people finally succumbed to something.

Hank entered the kitchen—dressed, clean-shaven, and his hair damply combed back. His face, its chiseled planes now even more defined, fit perfectly his grudging words of greeting. "Thanks for the nursing."

"You're welcome," she answered with stiff politeness, and poured a mug of coffee, putting it on the table next to his wallet.

So that's where it was. He pulled out a chair and sat down in front of it, an eyebrow lifting question-ingly when she moved the wallet slightly to place a plate of scrambled eggs and toast before him.

"When you finish eating, I'd like you to check the contents of your billfold, please. I used your money to pay the doctor the two times he was here. There are receipts, of course."

She continued doggedly in the face of his telling silence. "My job situation is not what I thought it to be or I would have paid him myself and *you* could have reimbursed *me,* for once."

He didn't smile at her small conciliatory joke. When did he ever? Instead of commenting, however, he merely gave her a cold look and picked up his coffee mug.

Gloria breathed again and Jamey buried his face in his milk glass, but his unblinking eyes never left Hank's face.

Above his coffee mug, Hank's chilly glance flicked over the boy and suddenly the milk glass jerked and Jamey spluttered. One ice-black eye had winked at him!

Gloria began to explain stiffly, "I...I couldn't help noticing that you carried a great deal of money and I—"

"I sold my car," Hank inserted, continuing to eat with his habitual single-minded economy.

She allowed herself to be diverted, remembering the battered early model Mustang sitting in her drive these last few days. Frowning in perplexity, she went to the stove to pour them both more coffee. "What was wrong with the other one?"

"Nothing. It was a great car."

Wow. Superlatives from the Great Stone Face? Then she frowned again. Maybe he needed the

money. Judging by the quality of his boots and un-
dergarments—and dishes…she sighed inwardly, eyeing the chip in the cup she held by its handle—he
certainly spent it on the oddest things. Yet he'd sold
a perfectly good though older model car for the only
slightly newer clunker in the driveway. The old Mustang had at least thirty tough years on it and had the
dents to prove it.

"It's a '65." Hank's drawl broke into her
thoughts. "I've been hoping to get my hands on one
like it for a long time. Everything on it came from
the factory."

Gloria hoped her opinion didn't show in her face.
Watching her, Hank grinned.

Her breath stopped. A smile like that should be
registered as a lethal weapon, she decided.

"What happened with the real estate office?" he
asked.

"The family plans to close it." She kept her voice
carefully neutral. "I wasn't notified because no one
knew I'd been hired. They're awfully sorry, but…"
She spread her hands expressively before her chin
came up again. "Guess I'll just have to find something else. It shouldn't be too difficult. I'm what's
known as a computer whiz. Now that Jamey is better,
I can go job hunting."

She paused, not liking the expressionless look on
Hank Mason's face. "Also, a substantial amount of
insurance money will be arriving any day now," she
added.

Hank stood abruptly and picked up his wallet.

Relieved, Gloria stood, also, to watch as he made
a cursory look through his possessions. Slowly he
counted five twenty dollar bills and two fifties onto

the table before his voice suddenly cracked into the quiet room.

"Now let's get down to business."

"You wait one minute, Mr. Mason—"

"And the first order of business is to dispose of the formalities. Jim here upchucked his cereal down my shirtfront and I woke up this morning in your bed without a stitch on. Under the circumstances, it seems silly to be calling each other Mr. Mason and Ms. Pellman. Wouldn't you agree?"

Gloria tilted her scarlet face to its proudest angle.

"The second order of business is the loan I'm making you."

"No!"

"Yes. Pride doesn't feed your kid, so listen up. This is business and nothing more. Philanthropy's not part of my nature. You said you have money coming even if you don't find a job, so sooner or later you'll be in funds. As soon as your refrigerator is full and next month's rent is paid, I expect repayment at twenty percent interest. If you decide to leave town you can send it to me care of General Delivery. If you don't send it, don't doubt for a second that I'll find you."

"No."

"Look, Glorie—"

"Twenty percent is too high for a short-term loan. I'll—"

"All right. Make it ten percent."

"Six."

His eyes glinted. "Eight."

"Done." Gloria stacked the money neatly and folded it.

"Would you like me to sign anything?" she

asked, but Hank, with a low growl, placed his Stetson on his head, pulled the brim low over his eyes, and picked up his sports bag. From the look on his face, she decided a written agreement wasn't part of Hank's plans.

He strode out the front door, leaving it to slam with an irritated bang behind him.

The Mustang's motor didn't turn over at once, but he babied it patiently until the car gathered courage and finally, accompanied by moans and groans and rattles, backed out of the driveway.

Gloria shook her head when the old car at last crawled around the corner and out of sight.

During the day Gloria found herself thinking of Hank at unexpected moments. The pictures conjured were odd ones—Jamey gripping Hank's thumb in his sleep; Hank's dangerous, devastating smile; the burst of infectious laughter accompanying a scene lived only by himself when fever had him in its grip; the slow steady pulse she had felt above her head at three in the morning as his fingers splayed in her hair.

"Just lonely, I suppose," he'd whispered, the words tearing into her heart to find a kindred echo.

Then there were the silk briefs he wore, a far cry from the utilitarian jockey shorts one would expect from such a no-nonsense man. Those sensuous scraps covering nothing but the essentials were enough to make the most jaded woman's heart stop.

Would she ever again be able to see him in his soft faded Levi's without remembering what he wore underneath? Or the way it felt to be held firmly against him when he wore almost nothing at all?

And who was Jane? An ex-girlfriend? A current lover perhaps? Twice Hank had rambled her name.

He was an enigma, Hank Mason was. Slinky underwear and antique silver, an outhouse, and Charley the spider. A quiet man who put himself out for no one willingly. Yet he had won over Jamey—a disturbed child who, since he was two years old, had allowed no one but his mother to touch him without having hysterics.

Gloria deftly mitered a sheet, tucking a corner under the mattress, then she lifted and flipped her blue spread and smoothed it over the bed without conscious thought.

Enough, she told herself sternly. Hank Mason is gone and good riddance. Time to start thinking about the job opportunities in Tulaca.

Two years of college toward a Liberal Arts degree didn't qualify her for much. Her college hours made her seem out of place to the people who hired in the nonskilled areas, and in the offices of the business world, the Liberal Arts courses meant nothing.

What little work history she had was also against her. She'd never worked until after she left Eric and since then the longest she'd held a job was three months. Eric would find her and Jamey and she'd be forced to move again. Finally he'd had the sense to obey the restraining order the court placed against him. But by then Jamey's bouts of hysteria had babysitters calling her away from work one too many times to be tolerated by a boss who expected his employees on the job during the designated hours.

But as she'd told Hank, she was a computer dynamo. There wasn't a computer manufactured that she couldn't eventually make sit up and dance, nor a manual written in the most arcane computereze that she couldn't decipher. She had the talent, but she didn't have the certificate or the college hours to prove it. Her skill was all intuitive, much like being able to play the piano by ear.

But would this town, dominated by the mountain in her front window, recognize and need that ability?

It didn't take long for Gloria to learn both the strengths and the drawbacks of small-town living. A city girl, she was unprepared for the fact there was no daily paper, only a weekly that came out on Thursdays. When she opened it and found that the classifieds took up no more than half the back page, with not a single Help Wanted ad among them, she felt a sinking sensation in her stomach.

Slowly she folded the paper in half and put it beside her coffee cup, watching Jamey as he pushed his small plastic truck along the "roads" formed by the squares in the scarred kitchen linoleum.

So what were her options?

At the moment, the necessities of food and shelter were met. Thanks to Hank, there was money in her purse, the meager remains of her savings now beefed up with a bit extra. It wouldn't last indefinitely, of course, but could she stretch it until the insurance money came or she found another job in Tulaca?

Or should she use it to go to another town? Jakerville, perhaps, where Hank said a chemical plant was under construction? Maybe the contractors needed someone with her computer skills.

Did she have enough money to move, find a place to stay, and still have something to live on while searching for a job, then wait for the first paycheck, assuming the insurance check didn't arrive in the meantime?

She doubted it.

Sighing quietly, Gloria picked up a piece of toast and munched it, the small action giving her time to think, to weigh the advantages of staying in Tulaca.

Her rent was paid through the month and the utilities were included in the rent. By not moving there was no call on her money except for expendable groceries like bread and milk. Financially, not moving was to her advantage, at least for the next month.

Okay, then. Tulaca was small, but that didn't mean there were no jobs. It just meant everyone knew everyone so advertising job openings wasn't necessary. Word of mouth was probably more efficient than the newspaper. Since Gloria didn't know anyone—except Hank Mason, and she doubted knowing him would be to her benefit—she would visit every business in town and inquire.

Ray Griffith at the lumberyard was sorry. He'd just hired office help last week.

Johnny Holt's wife kept the books for the garage.

The Roadhouse Steakhouse on the edge of town didn't need any waitresses right now and the variety store employed high school students in the vocational program.

The bookstore was a one-woman operation, as was Margo's Dress Shoppe. Raul's Mexican Food Restaurant employed only members of Raul's large family.

The Sunset Motel wasn't looking for help, but Sarah Swift, the motel manager, had heard that the Tulaca First Baptist Church needed a secretary.

Gloria called on the Reverend Bill Tyson and learned that yes, the church did need a secretary. Did she play the organ?

She blinked. "No, sir, but I type fifty words a minute on a typewriter and I can use any kind of computer."

Reverend Bill chuckled. "You see, Gloria...May I call you Gloria?"

At her dazed nod he continued. "We also need an organist and we're a poor church. We can't afford to hire two people so we're looking for one person to do double duty, so to speak. Twice the manpower for half the salary." He chuckled again. "If you know what I mean."

Gloria knew.

Wearily she trudged back to her little house, Jamey's hand in hers. Knowing no one to leave him with, she had taken the child with her as she searched for work. Now he walked silently beside her, his feet dragging. As Hank had noted, Jamey ought to complain more, but right now she was glad he didn't.

As if her thinking his name conjured the stone-faced mountain man, at that moment the Mustang rattled to a stop beside her. Jamey lit up like a neon light.

"Hank," the boy whispered. There was no fear in the soft voice, just gladness, but he didn't let go of Gloria's hand.

To make the door stay closed Hank had to slam it twice after he got out of the car. Gloria half smiled and shook her head, eyeing the elderly vehicle dubiously.

A faint light sheened his onyx eyes as Hank

watched her. "I've been looking for you," he said abruptly. "Hello, Jim."

His hand went out toward the boy and Jamey cringed. The hand kept coming, however, and one lean finger touched Jamey's nose.

"Yep, still there," Hank said easily, and something leapt in the boy's golden eyes.

Tentatively Jamey reached up and also touched his nose as if verifying the man's opinion. The small snubbed appendage wrinkled a bit and one side of his mouth quirked engagingly.

Fascinated by the small exchange, Gloria had forgotten Hank's words until his eyes swung back to her, their black depths now without expression. Her chin tilted to fighting position.

"Why were you looking for me?" she asked, her tone aggressive. "I haven't found a job yet. If you're needing your money..."

"I said," he interrupted, his tone determinedly mild, "I didn't want repayment until after you find a job, pay next month's rent, and have a full refrigerator. I meant it." The tone may have been mild but the words were chiseled in stone.

He continued, giving Gloria no time to speak. "I hear Reverend Bill at the Baptist Church is looking for a secretary. You might want to try there."

Gloria sighed. "I've just come from the parsonage. I don't play the organ."

One black eyebrow quirked.

"The church also needs an organist, but can't afford to hire two people. So Reverend Bill is looking for one person to do double duty, so to speak." She smiled faintly. "If you know what I mean."

Hank chuckled.

"Well," Gloria said, her tone as bright as she could make it. "Maybe I'll find something tomorrow. Job hunting is a good way to meet people anyway, and the people here seem very nice."

She avoided looking at him, gazing instead at the mountain looming in the near distance behind him. "Thanks for...for..."

"Butting into your business? Think nothing of it. It's a habit in Tulaca."

Immediately she drew herself up stiffly. "That's not what I—"

"That was a joke," Hank interrupted. "Do you want a ride home?"

"Mr. Mason, do you ever allow anyone to finish a sentence?"

He grinned the grin that always hit Gloria like an unexpected blow to the solar plexus. "Depends on the sentence. Do you want a ride home?" The repeated question held a mocking weary patience.

"No! I mean...no, thank you. It's only a couple more blocks." Jamey wiggled his hand a little and Gloria consciously loosened her clutch on the small paw.

Something in Hank's face said he'd seen the tiny movement, but he merely lifted two fingers to his forehead in a brief salute. "Okay. Break a leg...if you know what I mean. So long, Jim."

Involuntarily, Gloria laughed, the sound lost in the slam of the car door and the Mustang's rattle as he fired the ignition before easing the old car down the street.

Jamey looked into his mother's laughing face, liking it when she looked that way and not having seen it for a while. Yet he was troubled by Hank's words and his eyes darkened with anxiety. "Why does he want you to break your leg, Mama?"

Gloria reached out to touch the tip of his short nose in unconscious imitation of Hank's gesture. "It's just a grown-up's funny way of saying good luck," she explained.

"Oh." Jamey, too, touched his nose. "It's still there," he said.

"Yep."

Her son laughed, and after a moment of fighting tears of delight at the rare and precious sound, Gloria's watery merriment joined his.

She *must* find work in Tulaca. It was the home of Jamey's laughter.

Gloria had just finished tucking Jamey into bed for the night when she heard a car pull into her driveway, followed a few moments later by a soft knock at her front door.

Hank.

Automatically, she smoothed her hair and ran her hand around the inside waistband of her jeans to make sure her shirt was tucked in.

But when she opened the door, instead of Hank's tall lean frame, she found a small dumpling of a woman who looked like a Norman Rockwell grandmother.

The woman smiled. "Gloria?" she asked.

"Yes?" Gloria's voice held a city girl's caution at meeting strangers.

"I'm Martha Blackwell. My husband and I own Mom's Café on Main Street. May I come in?"

"Uh…yes, please do."

Gloria stepped aside to lead the woman to the di-

lapidated couch in the living room, secretly chagrined at the room's shabby state, though it was clean
as a new pin. Just as soon as she had extra money,
she vowed, and time....

"This place certainly is an eyesore," Martha
Blackwell commented, echoing Gloria's thoughts.
"Always has been. Needs somebody to love it, I
guess." She spoke without rancor or censure, and
smiled.

Drawn to the woman, Gloria smiled back, relax-
ing. "That's what I thought, too. May I get you a
cup of coffee, Mrs. Blackwell?"

"No, dear. I never touch it after the sun goes
down, but thank you anyway. Hank Mason says
you're a good cook."

Gloria's head came up sharply. "He does?" Since
when did the one bland breakfast she'd prepared for
him make the man an authority?

"He does. He also said you're looking for a job."

"Well yes, but..."

Mrs. Blackwell seemed not to have heard. "My
daughter, Arlene, lives in St. Louis," she continued,
apropos to nothing. "She's eight months pregnant,
you know."

"Oh. Um...you must be very proud."

"You didn't know. I'm sorry, dear. You don't
know what I'm talking about, do you? I forget sometimes that everyone's not hooked into the Tulaca
grapevine."

The older woman laughed comfortably. "Let me
start over. Mom's Café is looking for an interim cook
so I...I'm Mom, dear...can go to St. Louis to stay
with Arlene until she has her baby, then stay another

month to get mother and baby settled in. Now do you understand?''

Gloria laughed softly, enchanted with Martha Blackwell's mixture of puckish humor and practicality. "I think so. Are you offering me the job, Mrs. Blackwell?''

"Call me Mom, dear. Everyone does, even biddies older than I am. No, I'm not offering you the job, but I'm offering you the opportunity to come in and cook a meal for me. If you're as good a cook as Hank says you are, which means you're as good as I am, *then* I'll offer you the job.''

Frowning a little, Gloria replied slowly, "I've never cooked professionally, Mrs…Mom. Just for family and friends, and even then it wasn't anything fancy." In her past life, Eric had insisted that kind of thing be catered.

Mom's chuckle rolled up from her ample bosom. "Bless you, dear. You've never been into Mom's Café, have you?''

"I'm afraid not. I'm sorry.''

"That's all right. You'll get your chance tomorrow. That is, if you're interested. You see…'' She grinned at Gloria with a small round leprechaun's mischief. "Mom's specializes in home cooking. If you cook fancy, I don't want you." And she burst into laughter at her own joke.

Gloria laughed with her, thinking as she did so how much she had laughed today, even though up until now the day had been depressingly unsuccessful.

Perhaps Tulaca was the home of her laughter, too.

The next day she went to Mom's Café and prepared pork roast with all the trimmings. Mom and

Pop Blackwell sat down with Gloria and Jamey in one of the back booths to eat it as their noon meal.

To Gloria, the roast tasted like sawdust. She'd been far too liberal with the salt in the green beans and too stingy with it in the summer squash. The mashed potatoes were just a shade too lumpy and if only she'd left the fruit cobbler in the oven maybe three minutes longer.

When Mom and Pop finished eating and drained the last of their iced tea, they politely patted their mouths with their napkins and looked at each other.

Gloria's heart sank.

"Well, dear," Mom said at last, "that's the best meal I've had in a long time, outside one of my own, of course. You're hired."

Swallowing, Gloria blinked back tears. "Thank you," she said huskily. "When would you like me to start? I'll have to find someone to take care of Jamey."

She felt Jamey jerk in alarm beside her and her heart twisted, but it couldn't be helped. She had to work and Jamey had to learn to be away from her. "As soon as I get a sitter I can begin anytime you want me," she finished on a note of determination.

"Looks like your young one doesn't like the idea of a sitter much," Mom observed. "Would you like to stay with your mama, honey?" she asked the boy.

Jamey ducked his head but nodded emphatically.

Mom chuckled. "Do you see that swing set out in the yard?" She nodded out the side window to the fenced lawn between the restaurant and a large white frame house. "That's where my youngsters played when they were growing up and where my grand-children play when they come to visit."

Perking up, Jamey now looked out the window with interest.

"This is a family restaurant," she continued, speaking to Gloria. "People are used to my children and grandchildren being in and out. Won't matter any at all to have one more, as long as he doesn't run around, screaming and hollering. This is the family's booth and Jamey can nap here in the afternoons if you'd like, or use the table for games and such. And of course, the café supplies your meals."

With every word, the woman demolished Gloria's worries one by one. Again Gloria found herself trying to swallow an oversize lump in her throat. "You're the answer to a prayer," she said at last.

Mom's rich laugh bubbled forth. "No, dear. You're the answer to *my* prayers. Now I can go to St. Louis with a clear conscience. Pop's going to stay here and look after things. He's a dab hand at break-fast but he's no hand at all with dinner and supper. With you here, I don't have to worry that he'll poison anybody."

She began stacking their empty plates, not waiting for the waitress to bus their table. "Can you start this afternoon?" she went on. "If you and I work to-gether a couple of days before I go, I can show you where things are and teach you a few shortcuts I've learned over the years."

In the next few days Gloria learned that the res-taurant was closed on the weekends but during the week served three substantial meals of its choice

daily, the gist of which she was to print each morning
on a chalkboard near the entrance.

"Pop's writing is nothing but hen scratch," Mom
said, poking her husband's amply encased ribs with
a dimpled elbow.

Around outsiders, Mom was the talker and Pop the
listener, Gloria noticed, a state of affairs that seemed
agreeable to both of them. Yet when it came to com-
munication between themselves, Gloria saw how frequently Mom handed Pop the salt before he asked
for it, or Pop brought Mom a cup of coffee in the
middle of the morning and told her to put her feet
up.

One evening, after the three of them had closed
the café for the night, Gloria stood for a moment and
watched the Blackwells walk toward their house next
door, their quiet talk punctuated occasionally with
one of Mom's rolling chuckles. It floated back to
Gloria on the evening breeze and she saw that the
couple held hands.

That's what I want, she thought. A man who can
laugh with me. A man who will hold my hand while
we talk about our grandchildren, who will still be
holding my hand when our great-grandchildren come
to visit.

Hank Mason's craggy face filtered into her mind,
to be dismissed before it even seeped into conscious-
ness.

Two days later, Mom left for St. Louis.

Chapter Five

The work was easy.

Pop handled breakfast so Gloria didn't have to go in until nine in the morning to begin preparing the noon meal. A high school student helped with paring and chopping and cleaning up and Gloria often helped wait tables after the noon crush. Most of the early afternoon was given over to people who stopped in from their jobs for a quick coffee break and she usually handled this as Pop ran his errands or worked on the books, Jamey by this time napping in the back booth. By four, she was deep into preparations for the evening meal and by eight, home for the night.

Life was better than it had been in years. More important, Jamey thrived.

At first he sat in the back booth, big-eyed and still as people came and went in the café. But with his mother constantly in view and never seeming to mind when he claimed her attention for a moment, he gradually began to take an interest in the people who frequented Mom's Café.

Hank was one of them.

The first time Hank came in and saw Jamey sitting alone in the family booth, he came over to speak to him.

"Mind if I join you, Jim?" the man asked easily.

Jamey, unused to grown-ups asking *him* for permission to do anything, cautiously nodded his head. The booth was large so even with Hank in it he didn't feel threatened.

The boy didn't quite know what to make of this quiet man, but Hank had made him feel better when he was sick and hadn't gotten angry at all when Jamey vomited all over his shirt and promptly burst into tears. Hank had calmly cleaned them both up, then held the exhausted boy in his lap until he'd fallen asleep. When Jamey woke up sick again, Hank stood with him and they'd *both* thrown up into the commode. Jamey hadn't felt like such a baby, after all.

Yes, Hank could sit in the booth with him.

Gloria was in the kitchen, preparing the noon meal, and a waitress brought Hank his coffee. After she left, Hank leaned his head against the booth's tall backrest. "I'm a little tired, Jim." His drawl oozed out, slow and thick. "Do you mind not talking so much?"

Jamey wanted to laugh, but didn't quite dare. "Okay," he said shyly instead, but his eyes gleamed golden.

Hank drank his coffee and left, but after that he

often sat with Jamey when he came in, never failing to ask permission before doing so.

Frequently, other men joined them.

The first time this happened, a large heavy-set man sat down across from Hank on Jamey's side of the booth. Wilson, Hank called him. Jamey promptly scooted over so that a wide space existed between himself and the man.

Things were fine until Johnny Holt and another man came up to talk to Hank and then they, too, slid into the booth. This put Wilson smack up against Jamey, the wall on the boy's other side leaving him no further space to scoot.

He suddenly felt claustrophobic, and his heart began a sluggish pounding. Jamey swallowed, knowing that any minute now he was going to scream.

He didn't want to scream—he never wanted to, but the fear had a way of burying him under its waves until he had no choice but to scream or drown.

In his panic, Jamey's head lifted as he wildly searched for his mother. Instead his gaze collided with Hank Mason's craggy face.

Fear was black, like oil, thick and suffocating. But security was black, too, like twin magic stones whose gift was protection...a touch of magic belonging only to Jamey.

The fear, without even a scream to drive it away, slowly receded and Jamey watched, fascinated, as one lazy lid dropped over an onyx eye.

The boy smiled.

Gloria, finishing up in the kitchen for the afternoon, came to see if she could help in the dining room. When she saw the men crowded into the family booth her heart stopped.

Jamey!

How dare they! That booth was private. And there was Hank Mason, who should have known better. Yes, he sat with the boy sometimes, but it was just the two of them and Jamey knew Hank. But her son didn't like crowds.

More important, he didn't like men.

Unaware of her approach, none of the group looked up, except Hank whose black eyes watched her guardedly.

As well they should, Gloria thought waspishly, ready to break up this rooster party and free her son. Then she caught sight of Jamey, squeezed into his corner, dwarfed by a large man whose upper arm was about the size of the child's whole torso. Every protective instinct went into red alert.

Jamey hadn't seen his mother yet, but Gloria sensed the tenseness in his small body. He had scrootched up against the wall as far as he could get. Then she saw him lift his glass of milk and sip just as Hank lifted his coffee cup.

Why, he was pretending to be one of these men! she realised. He was still afraid, but for the first time Jamey was handling his fear.

She caught words like "piston" and "valves," "rpm's" and "voltage regulator." The tension eased from her body as if the words were as fascinating for her as they were for Jamey, and a great relief took its place.

Johnny Holt looked up at that moment. "Oh, hi, Gloria," he said genially. "Would you like to sit down?" He stood so that she could slide into the booth next to Hank.

"No, keep your seat, Johnny. I...um...thought

you fellows might like more coffee.'' Realizing then that she hadn't brought the coffeepot, she smiled quickly to the table in general. ''Be right back.''

When she returned, she refilled everyone's cup, even gravely adding a dollop of coffee to Jamey's glass of milk, turning it a light tan color, then left the men alone as if Jamey sitting with them was the most natural of events.

How, she wondered, had *that* miracle occurred?

After the men left, Hank lingered. He and Jamey sat quietly together in companionable silence for a few minutes. Then Hank focused his attention out the big window beside them.

''Nice day out,'' the man said at last. ''Lots of sunshine.''

Jamey, too, looked out the window. The grass in the Blackwells' lawn was lush and thick in the bright sunlight, dappled here and there by the shade of trees rustling their late spring leaves. But there was a sleepy quietness about the scene that seemed out of place somehow.

''That old swing set looks lonesome.''

Hank's soft drawl floated toward Jamey as the boy studied the empty yard. The words might have been part of his thoughts.

''Guess it misses having children to play with,'' Hank continued. ''If you get time, you might go out and cheer it up.''

Jamey turned to look at him, but Hank was fishing in his pocket for change to leave on the table. ''See you later, Jim,'' he said, and was gone.

After a moment Jamey whispered, ''Bye,'' then turned to look back out the window at the lonesome

swing set, sitting in dejected boredom in the som-
nolent sunshine.

He sighed softly.

A few days later Gloria was busing a table after a
group of coffee drinkers left when Jamey came running in the side door from the Blackwells' fenced
yard.

"I just saw Mr. Mason go by," the boy reported.

"Did you?" Gloria continued to stack dirty coffee
cups in the large plastic tub. Jamey seemed to think
he was supposed to tell her every time Hank drove
down the street.

The Reverend Bill and his wife, sitting at the next
table and out for a rare late lunch, looked at each
other.

"Yes," Jamey said, answering his mother's rhe-
torical question and a little miffed that she wasn't
more interested.

"You took care of Hank while he had the flu, I
understand," Mrs. Tyson said, having no qualms
about bringing into the open what the town knew
anyway.

Gloria flushed, beginning now to understand the
wonder of the Tulaca grapevine. "Um, I did. Yes.
You see, he was, well, baby-sitting Jamey when Jamey became ill. When Hank became sick, too, I
couldn't just let him leave after he'd been so kind to
Jamey."

"Hank Mason is a kind man," Mrs. Tyson replied
placidly. "There's few people in this town he hasn't
helped out at one time or another. It's a shame we
don't see more of him."

Wiping off the table with a damp cloth, Gloria
waited but it seemed Reverend Bill's wife wasn't go-

ing to continue. "Doesn't Hank live here?" she asked at last.

Mrs. Tyson was clearly delighted with the question. "Oh, no. He lives in Albuquerque. But sometimes he comes back to Tulaca and works with Johnny Holt in the garage. It's his way of taking a break from the city. He grew up here, you know."

Reverend Bill picked up the story. "And, boy, was he a wild one, if you know what I mean. Smoking, drinking, fighting. That boy *loved* to fight."

Gloria froze, but the reverend appeared not to notice. He chuckled reminiscently.

"And half the time truant from school. Every few days Sheriff Hazlett would get a call from the school to go up the mountain and get him. It's where he always went. That mountain's been Hank's favorite place ever since he was a little thing. We didn't know that when his sister died. The boy turned up missing for four days...had every man in town out looking for him. Then he comes walking off that mountain cocky as you please, dirty, hungry, and a chip on his shoulder a mile wide, so to speak."

"Well, what do you expect with Charlene Mason for a grandmother?" Mrs. Tyson asked her husband tartly.

"Hank was wild as Bill says," she then said to Gloria, knowing she had a fascinated listener. "But as he got older, he grew out of most of it. He was a reader, too. I was town librarian before I retired and Hank came in the library two or three times a week. Read everything he could get his hands on."

She smiled to herself a moment in fond remembrance before continuing. "Probably people forgave his wild ways because the boy helped anyone who needed it. Mowed old Mrs. Schaffer's lawn and wouldn't take a penny for it, even though he was poor as a church mouse. Fixed Gus Lucas's delivery truck when Gus couldn't afford to take it to the garage. Things like that.''

"But he always did things for people kind of back-handed-like, you might say," the Reverend Bill inserted. "Never asked anybody if they wanted something done, just did it and went about his business. Mrs. Schaffer would hear a noise, look out the window and there'd be Hank mowing the grass. Next thing you knew, he was gone or acted all snarly if she came out and tried to thank him."

He chuckled. "Gus, he called the sheriff first time he saw Hank with his head inside that old rattle-trap delivery truck of his. Ran outside and started ranting and raving about juvenile delinquents. Hank just kept on taking things out of the motor like Gus wasn't even around. By the time Hazlett got there, everything was back together."

"'It'll run now,' Hank says, calm as you please, and goes around, gets in the driver's seat and starts her up. Sure enough, it runs like a charm. 'I wouldn't have to fix it if you'd keep the oil changed,' Hank says to Gus and leaves.

"Hazlett asked Gus if he wanted to press charges, but Gus said he guessed not. Three thousand miles later, Hank shows up to change the oil. Made Gus hopping mad, but Hank did it anyway, and every three thousand miles after that. Gus always threw a fit, but after a while he got to where he just expected the boy to show up to hear it. Looked forward to those three thousand miles, I thought. Gus didn't have any family to fuss at, you see. Or if he did, he drove them all off. Anyway, when he died, he left the boy that old jalopy. I think Hank still has it in Albuquerque.

"He always did like trucks," the Reverend added reflectively. "I'd say Hank's done real well for himself, if you know what I mean."

"He drives a '65 Mustang," Jamey said, his young voice holding a touch of importance.

Gloria looked down at him in surprise. Her son was certainly coming out of his shell.

Reverend Bill beamed at the boy. "That Mustang's a sweet little car, don't you think?"

Jamey may have nodded in easy agreement but Gloria wondered how anyone could call that beat-up old relic "sweet." Hank Mason's taste in vehicles probably made him a good mechanic from necessity.

Hank bent over the inner workings of the Caddy, listening with only half an ear as the garage's usual hangers-on joked among themselves and offered him and Johnny useless advice.

A garage is to many men what a water puddle is to a kid, he thought. Put the hood up on an automobile, open the bay doors to the afternoon sunshine and pretty soon every man in town with nothing better to do will drift in.

But he enjoyed it, enjoyed the mental challenge of making an automobile work like it should, enjoyed listening to the masculine gossip and ribald jokes, though he seldom took part in either. To him, garage kibitzers were like having a radio on for background noise...soothing but mindless.

Johnny Holt's Garage was one of the reasons he came back to Tulaca when his long-suffering office staff needed him to take a break. He'd tried working at one of his garages in Albuquerque, but someone always got nervous or thought he was interfering. In Tulaca, however, among people he'd known for years, he was just another mechanic.

This time, for some reason, the garage didn't seem to be having its usual soothing effect. He'd been down-to-the-gut tired when he arrived at the mountain a few weeks ago, strung out and feeling like a rat on a treadmill. Yet he'd no sooner gone to his favorite place to wind down than there was the business with the Pellman woman. Then her plumbing. Then his illness.

Especially his illness.

He hadn't allowed anyone to *care* for him since he was seven years old, and needing it at thirty-five still rankled. Of all the people who could have done it, it had to be Gloria Pellman, a haughty little piece with her nose in the air and more stubborn pride than was good for her.

All in all, this trip to Tulaca was proving to be as tense as life in Albuquerque. If it wasn't for the boy....

There was something about that boy. Jim acted on the outside the way Hank felt on the inside when he was growing up. But Jim, like Anna, didn't know how to hide it.

Mystery surrounded the boy and his mother, with Jim scared to death half the time and Glorie full of hostility. He'd bet a dime a doughnut it had something to do with the kid's father. And he'd bet another dime the kid's father was hurting. Hank knew he would be if someone took his son away from him, especially one like Jim.

The kibitzers switched their attention from Johnny, giving the Wallace boy's Camaro a tune-up, to Hank, in the middle of replacing the water pump in Mrs. MacAfee's '49 Cadillac.

"That Gloria at Mom's Café is some looker, ain't she?"

The question, following his thoughts so closely, brought Hank out of his introspection. He didn't answer the obvious lead. Concentrating on maneuvering the pump into its tight-fitting position, he thought about it though.

Was Gloria a looker? He supposed so, now that she was filling out some. But he wouldn't call hers an obvious beauty. Except, perhaps, for her eyes.

And hair that kept a man awake nights.

Other than that, he hadn't noticed.

Yeah, right.

Undaunted by Hank's silence, Wade Cummings continued slyly, "Did'ja hear what happened with Mel Stanton? You know, the car salesman from Jakerville?"

Hank's grunt was noncommittal.

"He was in Mom's trying to put the move on Gloria, y'know?" The man laughed. "Now don't get upset, Hank. This was before Mel knew you was in the picture."

When Hank didn't answer, Wade went on with his story. "Anyway, he was tryin' to get Gloria to notice him, go out with him an' all that, an' she just keeps ignoring everything he says. Finally, I don't know what he said or did, but it musta got to her. Her head went back and she got that special look of hers. You know how she does."

Her Aztec princess look, Hank called it.

"Anyway, she says...and everybody in the place heard her...she says, 'Mis-ter Stanton,' all prissy-like. 'Mis-ter Stanton, I'd like your phone number.'"

Hank's fingers lined up the bolt holes automatically.

"Ol' Mel, he grins and winks at his buddy and takes out his fancy gold ballpoint to write his number on a napkin. He's busy writin' when Gloria lets him have it. 'When all the men in the world are dead, Mis-ter Stanton,' she says, 'an' I need my cesspool cleaned, I'll call you.' And she picks up that napkin, folds it neat as you please and tucks it into her pocket. Then she walks away and leaves him with his mouth open. I heard he ain't been back since."

The men in the shop laughed.

Hank, at last, exhaled.

"What's she like, Hank?" Ned Scuddy asked curiously when things quietened down again.

Hank didn't straighten from his bent position over the Cadillac's engine. "Who?"

Ned laughed. "Who do you think? The Pellman woman, of course. She anything like Cindy Ann over at Coffey's Bar?"

Hank took his head out from under the hood and glanced briefly at Ned. "Not so I noticed. Hand me that ratchet behind you, would you? The one with the long handle."

Finding the correct ratchet, Ned handed it to him but couldn't help pursuing his question. "What's she like then?"

But the black-eyed stare that suddenly fixed on him instantly killed his curiosity.

"Guess you'll have to find that out for yourself,"

Hank answered, the mildness of the reply only enhancing its danger.

"Got a death wish, Ned?" Wade asked, grinning.

"No, sir. Not me. Uh-uh." Ned raised his hands and took an exaggerated step back.

The men laughed and even Hank's mouth tilted up a little.

"We're all goin' over to Coffey's later this evenin', Hank. You comin' with us?"

"Might." Hank examined his work under the hood critically. "Why don't one of you layabouts try to talk Mrs. MacAfee into getting a new car. Tell her it's un-American to have only one in a lifetime."

He wiped his hands on an oily rag before bending over the motor again. "I think I've replaced everything in this old crate at least twice. Parts for a '49 Caddy are getting hard to find."

His grumbles weren't typical, but no one seemed to notice. As the conversation turned to the Japanese auto industry, and then to how the Braves were doing this year, Hank went back to the water pump.

A month after Hank loaned the money to her, Gloria trudged up the mountain to pay it back, the folded bills resting firmly in the pocket of her new jeans.

She was full of good feeling this morning. The summer sun, already intense in Tulaca, merely filtered through the tall pines bordering the dirt road. Intermittent birdsong serenaded them on their way and she laughed when Jamey tried to whistle back.

There were no houses and they met no cars, so when Hank's cabin came into view a couple hours later, it looked as still and silent and aggressively independent as its owner.

Gloria remembered the first time she had seen it, when she'd walked up the mountain with Jamey after their arrival from Texas. Then she had thought the cabin looked lonely. Now she knew it was just alone, unneedful of the companionship of neighbors. Hank Mason didn't need or want anyone.

The Mustang was parked to the side of the cabin with its hood up, a constant state of affairs, she surmised, remembering its asthmatic rumblings. Sure enough, when she drew closer she saw Hank in front of it, bent over and fiddling with the mysterious inner works of the motor. He showed no surprise at her sudden appearance, merely straightened and began cleaning grease from his hands with a rag placed for the purpose on a front fender.

"Hello, Glorie."

Damn him. When he called her that, the only person in her life ever to do so, her toes curled.

"I believe we had a business agreement," she replied stiffly. "A part of which was the use of correct first names."

He gave her a mocking tilt of his head in acknowledgement. "So we do. Hello, Glorie. Hello, Jim."

"Glori-ah," she enunciated. "My son's name is Jamey."

"My name is James," her son corrected her gravely, but with a decided note in his voice she had never heard before. "I like to be called Jim." He looked up at the man now standing before him. "Hello, Mr. Mason."

"My name is Henry, Jim, but I like to be called Hank." With solemn courtesy the two shook hands, excluding Gloria completely from this male ritual.

Then Hank shifted his attention to her. "Would

you like a glass of water? You both look a bit wilted around the edges.''

Gloria gritted her teeth. ''Thank you.'' The blasted man had just made her feel like a perspiring dishrag.

Hank led the way into the cabin and held the screen door for his guests, a light glinting far back in his eyes. It took next to nothing to get this woman's back up and this time he hadn't even been trying.

Yes, she was a ''looker'' now, he thought, remembering the gossip in the garage and surveying the trim bottom outlined by her new jeans as Glorie passed in front of him.

She and her son were a far cry from the bedraggled pair he'd first seen. A few added pounds, new clothes, and a fresh healthy glow about them both made quite a difference. Her hair was still wild and free, untamable he'd bet, but shining like black watered silk in the bright sunlight of the meadow. No, in his opinion she would never be pretty, but she had all the makings for being beautiful.

Gloria Pellman would have half the male population of Tulaca and the surrounding area camped on her doorstep if she'd just say the word, but the boy didn't need that kind of life. It was probably just that sort of thing that made him such a shy little rabbit.

The woman's mistake had been in turning down dates in the beginning. She didn't know that in the town's eyes her refusal to go out with anyone made her indisputably Hank's property.

For the boy's sake he'd see that it stayed that way.

As the two drank his water, sparkling and cold from the well, he eyed the obviously new nylon backpack on Glorie's shoulders. ''You might as well take off the pack,'' he said when she put her empty glass in the sink. ''It looks heavy.'' The woman's nose shot in the air.

Hank gave a small resigned shake of his head, which only made her chin jut forward.

Lord!

''It's not heavy and we're not staying. I only came to repay the loan you gave me.''

''We're having a picnic,'' Jamey informed him as Gloria reached into her back pocket for the money. She counted it out on the table much as Hank had done originally.

''Here is your two hundred dollars and your interest. I believe that makes us even but you can count it if you like. I'll be glad to make up the difference.''

''May I say hello to Charley?''

Jamey's question gave Hank time to swallow the curse ready to leap into the air.

''He's in the same place, boy. Still doesn't talk much, though.''

He waited until the child left before gathering the money from the table with cold precision to place the bills in his wallet and dropping the change into the front pocket of his jeans. ''You're an irritating woman, sweetheart.''

She came right back at him. ''You're an irritating man, darling.''

His lips twitched, though he didn't smile.

Gloria Pellman was quick, he had to admit, the only woman he knew in Tulaca willing to stand up to him verbally. She took his cynical endearment and twisted it back on him in spades. Admittedly, his weren't love words but, like Marina, was that her specialty, using a man's softer feeling against him?

Come to think of it, she'd never explained Jim's absent father.

"Are you divorced, Ms. Pellman?"

The question came so unexpectedly that Gloria answered without thinking. "Yes."

"Does your ex-husband know where you are?"

"That's none of your business."

Perhaps not, Hank thought, but I'll bet the man's hurting for his kid.

"He doesn't know where you are and therefore he can't see his son. He's been trying to see Jim, hasn't he? And that's why you left Houston."

"I repeat. That's none of your business. Back off."

But Hank couldn't back off, all the pain of lost family coming to the surface at the thought of how he'd feel if Marina had taken a son like Jim away from him.

"You're smother-loving a perfectly nice kid just to take out some kind of perverted anger on your ex-husband," he said bitterly.

Gloria's hands clenched into impotent fists at her sides. "You have no right to sit in judgment of me," she whispered in breathless rage. "You know nothing about my life. Jamey's father is dead! He was killed a few months ago in an automobile accident."

As if she'd punched him in the gut, Hank actually took a short step back. Suddenly all sorts of anomalies about this woman fell into place. Insurance money. He'd never even thought of *life* insurance! And ex-wives frequently still loved ex-husbands.

He ran a hand through his hair and turned away from her. "I didn't know. I'm sorry," he said stiffly, feeling like a heel.

"You don't need to be."

Her bitter response jerked his head around and he stared at her incredulously.

She glared back at him, golden eyes glinting through a faint sheen...and she shook over every inch, a small forlorn leaf trying desperately to cling to its branch in a gale.

"Ah, Glorie," Hank said hoarsely, and gathered her into his arms.

"Don't touch me!" Her voice came high and shrill as she stiffened. But the strong arms wrapped around her shoulders anyway. Lifting her head, she silently, desperately fought the sudden urge to yield to the too comforting embrace and began instinctively to struggle against it.

Then she caught sight of Hank's face.

All the gentleness in the world formed the lines of that stone visage and she remembered suddenly a boy long ago, with a smile that told her everything in her small world was all right once again, and who knelt in front of her with a tabby kitten nestled in his hand.

"Don't touch me," she whispered again, and buried her face in his waiting shoulder.

For long moments Hank cradled her against him, not understanding why Glorie quaked like a mountain aspen, knowing only that she did and he couldn't stand it. One hand held the back of her head and he lowered his face so that a cheek rested against her forehead, as if to shield her quivering body with his own.

They stood quietly for an eternity of time until gradually her trembling stilled. She sighed, a soft whuffling of breath that warmed his skin through his shirt...a warmth that traveled slowly, inexorably to all the wrong places.

Lifting his face, Hank stared down at the small dark head below, even as his arms pulled her more tightly against him, so that her breasts were radiant heat against his chest. Her arms encircled his waist as if that were their natural resting place and the awareness of her snugged against him swelled and stirred the area that it pressured.

Gloria's head lifted slowly, pulled by invisible strings.

Thought stopped. Breathing shallowed.

Until Hank's face, magnet attracted to magnet, bent to hers.

Until Gloria's face, flower to sunshine, raised to his.

Until lips touched lips. Parted.

Touched again. Opened.

And being exploded into total sensuality.

On tiptoe, Gloria stretched higher, seeking. Hank's mouth was soft, softer even than the last time it claimed hers in a kiss she'd been trying for weeks to forget. His lips now played over her own like warm honey. Sweet, she thought. So very, very sweet.

Hands cradled her gently and she found her open eyes looking into the downsweep of long, softly curling lashes. Her own fanned slowly down as velvet warmth spread throughout her body, her mouth and tongue seeking more and more of the wild honey Hank had so much of, her hands holding his head, her fingers in his dark straight hair.

Mouth to mouth, body to body. She felt his hands running over her back, bracketing her breasts. The heat of his hands was her heat, and the press of his mouth ignited the fuel of life.

If she could, she would crawl into his warm darkness and shut the world out. Wrapped inside him, she would wrap him inside her. She would....

Gloria jerked back, eyes wide with shock.

"No," she whispered in horror, then screamed, "No! Let me go. I can't! I won't!" In a frenzy of fear of what he did to her, she began to fight him, hitting at every part of him she could touch.

Stunned, Hank wrapped her in the bear hug, his favorite form of defense. "Glorie, dammit. It was only a kiss. Stop it!" But the struggling woman in his arms was past listening.

Holding her flailing, squirming body, Hank gazed past her shoulder at the cabin's far wall without seeing it. How the hell had this happened? he wondered dazedly...just as the high keening cry of an animal in torment filled the room.

Jamey.

Chapter Six

Jamey!

Gloria stopped fighting abruptly, appalled at what her son had witnessed. Oh, God, don't let it start again, just when he'd been doing so much better.

Hank let her go, and the wildly sobbing child grabbed her hand. ''Run, Mama! He'll hurt you! Run!'' he gabbled before his screams escalated into incoherency.

Gloria, on her knees now, tried to take Jamey into her embrace, but the child was beside himself, twisting and crying mindlessly.

Finally, Hank squatted, gently shouldered Gloria aside, and took Jamey into the same bear hug he had just used on the child's mother. He stood, the struggling, screaming bundle wrapped firmly in his arms, and walked to the door, Gloria following after him.

At the door, however, he turned to face her

squarely. "This is my fault, Glorie. My holding you like that frightened him. Leave him with me for a few minutes."

He stared down into her pale wet face and something in it must have given consent because, turning once more, he walked out the door, seemingly oblivious to the writhing child in his arms.

Crossing her arms to grip her shoulders tightly, Gloria watched him go.

Hank went no farther than the front porch. Gloria watched through the screen door as he sat on the wooden step, still holding Jamey in that all-encompassing hug, the child's terrified screams echoing over the meadow.

Leaning slightly sideways so that his back rested against one of the posts supporting the porch, Hank merely sat silently, as if he had all the time in the world, the arms cradling the boy remaining solidly secure and embracing.

Gradually the screams and flailing weakened into tired, limp sobs. Still Hank made no attempt to soothe the boy, but held him close until Jamey stopped crying abruptly, his eyes growing enormous in his wet face.

"I hear your heart thumping," the child said with surprise, and Hank chuckled down into the golden eyes looking back into his with such wonder. He ran his hand over the bright hair, smoothing it away from the mottled, overheated face.

"Well now, Jim," he said in the slow, rich drawl so at odds with the sharp planes of his countenance. "Are you feeling better?" He shifted Jamey so that he now sat on his lap and the boy leaned trustingly against him, his head just under Hank's chin.

''Yes,'' Jamey whispered, and snuffled.

Hank reached into his back pocket and brought forth his large handkerchief and handed it to him.

Gloria left her place at the door and went back into the kitchen area. Jamey's escalation into hysteria had been a shock, but nowhere near the shock of his capitulation to Hank's rough brand of charm.

What was there about the man that caused her untrusting son to trust? Hank seldom smiled, made no concessions for the child's youth or size, yet Jamey clearly idolized him.

Though Hank had taken the blame for the boy's panic, Gloria knew it was her own behavior that had frightened him. Jamey had no way of knowing his mother was overreacting to what was only a kiss, after all. Hadn't Hank said so?

And it hadn't been fear of Hank Mason that sent her into a tailspin—it was fear of herself. Hank's kiss stirred into life what she thought Eric had surely killed.

Hoped he'd killed.

She didn't want a man in her life. She didn't *need* a man in her life. Especially one like Hank Mason.

The low exchange of voices continued on the front porch and she decided to make herself at home and make a pot of coffee. Her frazzled nerves could use a slug of caffeine and she needed to be *doing* something.

Jamey and Hank came into the cabin, walking side by side, just as the coffee finished perking. Both of them looked subdued. Gloria's hands clenched into nervous fists once more.

''I've been invited on a picnic,'' Hank said easily. ''We can pour that coffee into something and take it with us." He paused a moment. "I was also told to apologize. I'm sorry I upset you, Glorie."

He gazed unsmilingly down into her face, obviously waiting for her answer, his black eyes hidden as usual behind the shadow of his lashes and high angled cheekbones.

Gloria stared back at him militantly, all of her protective antipathy rushing back. She opened her mouth...and caught sight of her son's tear-stained, but now brightly expectant face.

Her mouth snapped shut and she visibly swallowed back the sharp words ready to leap off her tongue. "Apology accepted," she managed to choke out.

Something in the lift of Hank's brow said he could read her mind, and she turned away from him to pour the fresh-perked coffee into the vacuum bottle he provided. When he left the cabin to close up the Mustang, she sighed quietly with relief.

Finding a towel on a hook she wet a corner of it and washed Jamey's face, then the two of them hugged each other in mutual silent commiseration.

Hank had just lowered the hood on the automobile when Gloria and Jamey left the cabin. He gave them a brief look without speaking, set off across the meadow and angled toward the road, leaving them to trail through the tall, sweet-smelling grasses in his wake.

Her stride stretched and quickened when they reached the dirt road and Jamey was trotting when Gloria stopped abruptly, mutiny and heat suffusing her face. Folding her arms over her heaving chest, she glared at the broad back some way ahead of her. "Hank Mason, I will not follow behind you like a galloping puppy. You can slow down or picnic by yourself.''

The man stopped and turned slowly to face her in innocent surprise. ''Jim seems to be keeping up just fine, Glorie.''

''Jamey,'' she said through clenched teeth, ''is running. A picnic is a leisurely affair, not an endurance race.''

After glancing down at the sweat-streaked, red-faced boy right at his heels, without a word Hank lifted the child and swung him onto his own broad shoulders.

Jamey immediately took a compulsive fistful of Hank's thick hair, but quickly realized the advantage of this high perch and gazed around with interest.

''Wow!'' he breathed softly, and Gloria, who had joined them by now, laughed up at him.

Holding Jamey's ankles together in front of him with one large hand, Hank used the other to reach up and loosen Jamey's grip in his hair. The boy switched his clutch to under the man's chin. Then, with the young arms embracing his head, Hank reached out and took Gloria's hand as naturally as if he'd been doing it for years before setting out once more, following the road as it led higher up the mountain.

The clasp, she found, was unbreakable, but she now had no trouble keeping up with him.

When the road narrowed to little more than a track, Hank left it and turned off into the trees where he swung Jamey to the ground again. Here they walked single file, with Gloria conscious of the extraordinary noise she and Jamey seemed to make as they followed Hank as he moved through the woods with his usual silence.

Walking behind him, she had ample time to admire the way the man ahead of her slipped through the trees with the lean grace of a mountain cougar, a wiry, muscled strength to him that told of an active outdoor life, not visits to a gym—the kind of strength that would last a lifetime, and shelter all whom he loved.

The thought filtered through her mind with the gossamer tendrils of woodsmoke, surprising her.

Yet did Hank even know how to love? she wondered. Except for his potent kisses, he seemed incapable of the emotion. But had he ever been other than the hard, cynical man he was now? Was there once a time when he loved with the freedom of impetuous youth?

Jane perhaps?

They emerged from the trees into an open area bounded on one side by a sheer drop of several thousand feet, opening a vista of space and grandeur with range after range of mountains fading in limitless shades of purple into the distance.

Gloria breathed in sharply at the majestic beauty spread before her, knowing in that moment why she had dreamed of mountains over the last three years as she struggled with a world shifting beneath her feet. She stood for long silent moments breathing in the view.

Finally she turned to Hank, the joy dying in her eyes as a rare trace of apology took its place.

"It's a lovely spot, Hank," she said, her voice gentle. She might have been turning down a gift inappropriately too expensive. "But we can't picnic here."

The response came coated with frost. "Why not?"

"It's not a place for children," she answered quietly. "If Jamey went too near the edge…" She shuddered.

Jamey tugged her hand to get her attention. "The rocks fall if you go too near the edge," he told her matter-of-factly. "So I stay near the trees. Only Hank is safe 'cause the eagle watches out for him."

Gloria gazed down at her son in astonishment and even Hank looked momentarily nonplussed.

"The eagle told Hank I was here when the squirrel led me to him and then it told Hank to move so he wouldn't fall when the rocks did."

The unaccustomed spate of words died abruptly as Jamey looked around with a small satisfied smile. "I'm hungry, Mama." He sat down and leaned against a tree trunk.

Gloria turned to look up blankly into Hank's impassive face.

"This is where Jim found me when you fell and knocked yourself out," he replied, offering no other enlightenment. He slid the pack from his shoulder to lower it to the ground beside Jamey before dropping in an easy fluid motion to sit next to the boy.

"Looks like you're outvoted, Glorie," he said quietly, and smiled up at her.

Trapped by magic, she sat.

Hank winked at Jamey. "The eagle isn't going to allow Jim to do anything foolish."

Hoping her movements concealed the fine tremor in her hands, a direct result of that devastating smile, Gloria removed from the pack the plastic container of ham and cheese sandwiches she had made that morning. There was another of corn chips, a couple of apples, and a small flask of lemonade. She had also brought two old towels that she spread for herself and Jamey to sit on, but her son followed Hank's example and opted for the needle-covered earth.

Jamey, munching the last of his apple, suddenly exclaimed softly, "There's your eagle, Hank. He's looking for you."

Hank's gaze followed the small, pointing finger to the eagle riding the silent currents of air.

Gloria, looking at his hard, impassive face, had the feeling Hank wasn't with them at all, his spirit out there soaring with the eagle's, two wild things sharing secrets that shut out the puny world of man.

His words, when they came, seemed to echo her thoughts. "It's not my eagle, Jim. He belongs only to himself."

There was a moment of silence and then he smiled suddenly into the boy's face. "And he's not looking for me. He's looking for lunch. Even eagles get hungry."

Jamey surveyed the now empty containers that had held their own lunch. "I should'a saved a san'wich."

Pouring a cup of coffee into one of the metal cups from the flask, Hank leaned comfortably against the trunk of a pine. "Ham and cheese are much too tame for an eagle," he drawled. "A plump little rabbit, now…"

Gathering the empty containers and placing them in the pack, Gloria listened as Jamey's questions led from the eating habits to the nesting habits of the magnificent birds.

After a while she walked away from the quietly

talking pair. Jamey had stretched out on one of the towels and, judging by his heavy lashes, would be asleep soon. Would Hank be insulted to find he had put his small listener to sleep?

A group of boulders provided her with a seat and a backrest and she settled herself, facing the panorama of sky and mountains before her, feeling at once small and insignificant yet strangely at peace. Hank, when he came to settle himself on the ground beside her, gave an odd sense of completion to the scene.

Glancing over her shoulder Gloria saw Jamey curled up on the towel, napping peacefully as if all were right in his small world.

"Mountains seem to have a way of cutting a person down to size, shaving off the nonessentials till we're down to the bare bones of our weaknesses…and our strengths."

The quiet drawl was a part of the brisk breeze whipping her hair to the side, cooling the kiss of the summer sun where it caressed the strong planes of her face.

She felt no compulsion to answer, Hank's words merely the outward expression of her own thoughts, their perfect tuning not something of wonder.

Silence hummed peacefully between them for a while on the low keening of the wind and Gloria rested her head against the rock behind her, closed her eyes, and raised her face to the sun.

"I'm sorry, Glorie."

She stiffened, her peace shattered by this reminder of the scene in the cabin.

"I apologized at the cabin because Jim wanted it,"

Hank added quietly. "I'm apologizing for myself now."

Gloria straightened, to stare determinedly at the vista spread before them. "I've already accepted your apology. I wish you'd just drop it."

"Your husband hit you, didn't he? That's why you're so afraid, why Jim is so nervous. Jim didn't say a lot, but I picked up enough to know he was scared to death of his father and so were you."

Pridefully stiff and straight, she sat forward, hands clenched in her lap. Hank had spoken to the distant mountains without facing her, and now she did the same, not looking at the black crown of his head where he sat just below her on the ground. Anger, buried so long under the weight of day-to-day responsibilities for herself and her young son, roughened her voice.

"I'm not afraid of anyone anymore," she all but growled. "I can give as good as I get. It took me two long years to learn that lesson, but when I did, I learned it well. Yes, Eric hit me and in the beginning I was afraid of him. But I loved him. Afterward, he was always so sorry. I thought if I just stayed with him long enough we could work things out. We lived in a beautiful house in one of Houston's better suburbs. Eric was CEO for an international firm and we were the typical upscale couple enjoying life at the top. But when Eric's problems at work coincided with some silly domestic upheaval, he took it out on me."

Unconsciously, her tone began to moderate, but her gaze still clung to the distant mountains.

"I loved him, but I couldn't live with his abuse, and had made up my mind to leave him when I discovered I was pregnant. That seemed to change everything. Eric began treating me as if I were made of porcelain and I thought perhaps my pregnancy was a turning point, that now we could make a stable life for ourselves. But when Jamey was three months old, Eric went after me with a belt buckle because the baby spit up on his suit jacket. In his mind, Jamey and I had teamed up to insult him. For some reason I retaliated with a broom handle. It was awful, a scene right out of a depressing film, but it worked, possibly because Eric allowed it to work. In his own way, I think, he loved me."

She stopped, took a chance, and looked down into Hank's unsmiling face, to find the bright sun had chased away its usual shadows, leaving the obsidian eyes exposed to her scrutiny. They told her nothing of his thoughts, however, for there was nothing but her own reflection in their black depths.

Somehow her hand had found its way into his.

"But you did leave. Is that when you came here?"

"No," she answered slowly, as if talking to herself in the reflection of his eyes. "As long as I stood up to him, Eric left me alone. It's not easy to break up a family and I suppose I fooled myself into thinking things were all right. Then I started finding bruises on Jamey. I thought they were accidents until one day I caught Eric pinching him. I left that very moment and immediately sued for divorce. There are organizations that do a wonderful job of helping battered women and children. One of them helped me, loaned me money to make the necessary changes. But Eric kept finding me...." She paused. There was no point now in going into that.

"Once he stopped using physical abuse," she said

instead, "Eric began using child support payments as a power play. That's why Jamey and I looked so...scruffy...when we arrived in Tulaca. There was never enough money and Jamey's hysteria made it difficult for me to keep a job." She swallowed. "We...we had to take a lot of charity."

The wind whispered through the small silence.

"Then Eric was killed in a traffic accident two months ago. It's ironic, I suppose. After years in the hell of wondering where next month's rent is coming from because he waited until just before the law was ready to go after him to pay Jamey's child support, Eric's death left Jamey and me financially secure." She smiled ruefully. "If the insurance checks ever get here."

Hank felt his heart clinch at that small smile.

"He never got around to changing the beneficiary on his policies, you see. Or maybe he never meant to. As I said, in his own way I think he loved us. But whether he did or not, I'll see to it Jamey grows up thinking he did. Every child deserves the love of his parents. I just hope someday Jamey can forgive his father."

Beside Gloria, Hank sat silently, unmoving.

"Jamey and I *needed* to get out of Houston," she continued. "A week after Eric's funeral, it seemed a minor miracle to see an ad in the paper looking for office help with computer skills and to find out the job was in Tulaca, the home of my happiest memories as a child. Within three months after we left here the summer you rescued my kitten, my father was dead. I always thought of that summer as my father's last gift to me."

Once more she lifted her eyes to the glorious vista

and finished simply. "Now I want to give the same gift to Jamey, only instead of an ending, it will be a new beginning."

Hank's thumb rubbed absently over the rounded nails of her fingers for a moment. "What about you? Have you forgiven Eric? Is Tulaca also a new beginning for you?" he asked quietly.

Gloria's attention shifted from the splendor of the mountains to the movement of Hank's thumb as she searched for words to express herself without excessive emotion.

She pulled her hand gently from his light grasp.

"Eric was sick. I know that. The judge denied him child visitation privileges until he could show proof of psychiatric counseling, but he made no attempt to get it. I can pity him now that he's dead. But I can't stand the thought of being dominated by any man in any way. Quite honestly, I don't know if I'll ever be ready to begin emotionally again. To trust completely again."

Hank stood then and walked to the edge of the cliff, standing for a long moment looking out over the earth just beyond the toes of his moccasins. The eagle had flown long since, the sky now empty even of clouds, and a bright summer blue that darkened to mauve where it touched the distant peaks.

When the man standing so rigidly with his back to her inhaled deeply, Gloria suddenly realized he fought tremendous anger, an anger evident only in the rapidly beating pulse in his clenched jaw as he turned once more to face her.

Slowly he walked back to her and this time joined her on her stone, hands clasped loosely before him, arms resting on his knees so that the back of his head with its longish cap of hair was all that she could see of him.

"Right now if your ex-husband was alive," he said softly, not looking at her, "I'd kill him...or at least give back to him all the hurt and fear he dished out to you and Jim."

The chill in his voice sent a sliver of fear down Gloria's spine.

"You're a better person than I to find pity for a man who harms those weaker than himself," Hank continued. "To some extent, I suppose everyone has a level of violence in them." He smiled wryly. "I can relate to that easily. But the world is full of out-lets. You slam things if you can't verbally attack and Jamey daydreams because he hasn't learned the fine art of yelling bloody murder with the other kids. Some people do push-ups or math problems, or...or other things."

Something in his voice alerted her and without thinking she reached out and pulled on his arm until his back rested on the stone with hers and she could see his face.

"What about you, Hank? What do you do?"

"When I'm angry or troubled I come to this place." He gestured to the view of space and dis-tance, mountains and sky. "Usually, whatever is wrong looks pretty silly when I take it out and ex-amine it up against that."

He found great interest in a cloud being born over a distant peak.

Instinctively, Gloria knew there was more. "And?"

"Well, sometimes, just for the hell of it and to let off steam, I go looking for a fight. When I was younger, I'd find the meanest bar in town where violence like mine is a way of life. Now, I find the nearest boxing gym where the fighting is more stylized and the referees are sober.''

The confession came stiffly and with a hint of apology. Clearly, in the face of her past, Hank thought Gloria would be shocked, perhaps even frightened.

She laughed softly and his head swung around, one brow lifted in inquiry.

"Fighting between equals and without anger isn't something I'd do myself,'' she explained, "but it's something I can understand.'' She grinned at him. "I'll bet you don't lose many of those fights,'' she added slyly. "One good cold-eyed stare is probably enough to freeze the competition.''

He laughed then, the hard planes of his face rearranging into laughter lines. He looked young and boyish and carefree, making Gloria laugh in answer, the sound of their mingled merriment forming soft music in the clear mountain air, rippling off rocks and trees and echoing back to them.

Hank looked into Gloria's shining eyes.

Caught, she looked back at him.

The laughter filtered away in the breeze, leaving behind a breathless hush.

"That's the first time I've heard you laugh,'' she said with soft wonder.

"You don't laugh much, either. Do you suppose we're a pair of curmudgeons?'' Hank asked huskily.

"I hope not,'' she whispered. Unconsciously she lifted her face closer to his as his hands threaded through her wildly flying hair to hold her head. His face filled her mind, her vision…

"Are you gonna kiss my mama again?"

Gloria started and would have pulled back, but Hank kept her head in his hands as he answered Jamey easily. "Yes, I am, Jim. Is that all right with you?"

Jamey shifted to the other foot and put one hand on Hank's knee, frowning. "Will she cry?"

Hank looked down into Gloria's pink-stained face and examined it seriously. "I don't think she will this time, but if she doesn't like it, I'll stop. Okay?"

Gloria didn't know if the question was for her or Jamey, but she nodded mutely.

She heard Jamey's soft, "Okay," as the mouth she'd been waiting for finally came home, touching down softly, as delicate and light as a butterfly, as sweet as the first scent of wildflowers in spring. The mouth that for the second time that day tasted of a soul's lost joy, and then...

And then vanished, leaving her bereft and cold and wanting more.

The black eyes looking into hers disappeared into shadow, unreadable, withdrawn. Hank's hands smoothed her hair briefly before he drew away from her. She took in a long, deep breath.

Jamey's face turned up to hers anxiously. "Did it hurt, Mama?"

"It didn't hurt at all, honey," she assured him and was pleased that her voice held only the trace of a wobble.

"Never had my kisses analyzed by a kid before," Hank growled, but Jamey thought it a nice friendly growl. "C'mon, Jim. I'll show you where an owl I know hangs out."

They walked away toward the trees, leaving Gloria on her perch in the rocks. She sat a moment, then walked to the spot where Hank had stood earlier, wrapping her arms around herself as the wind blew her hair wildly around her face.

Hank's kiss might have been her first, full of sweetness and a hint of exciting things to come. It didn't wipe out completely the sordidness and pain of the past, but it did acknowledge the emotional strength her past had given her.

Perhaps she could start over after all.

But not, she told herself immediately, with a mountain man. Even if he *was* a terrific kisser.

Turning, she walked swiftly toward the trees, following the voices of Hank and her son.

They left not long after and when they returned to the cabin Hank put them in the Mustang to take her and Jamey back to Tulaca.

To Gloria's surprise, the Mustang started on the first try, but the car's interior remained a disaster, seat covers ripped, carpeting torn and stained; an odor of mildew permeated the whole. She thought of the rich interior of the '56 Chevy with a puzzled sigh. Hank's excellent taste apparently didn't extend to the cars he chose to drive.

As he had the first time, when they arrived at her small house Hank took her key to first check inside, noticing as he did so the neatly cut lawn and trimmed shrubbery.

Nothing, however, could disguise the blistered paint of the front door. He opened it and stood looking around for a long, silent moment.

Gloria, standing behind and below him on the step, couldn't suppress a grin as she turned to wink at Jamey over her shoulder. At last Hank stepped farther into the living room, enabling her to come in behind him, and she, too, proudly surveyed her home.

The windows sparkled cleanly in the late afternoon sunshine, so that bright rays filtered through starched white curtains to pool on wood flooring waxed to a high gloss. A colorful patchwork throw covered the couch, its sagging contours hidden by a multitude of throw pillows made from an old sheet and brightly embroidered in her own patterns. The bare wall had been cleansed of all washable dirt, the various protruding nails removed, then its dinginess covered by a hanging she had designed and appliquéd with fabric scraps. Plants, from cuttings given to her by customers proud of their green thumbs, were everywhere.

Hank quickly checked the kitchen, the bedroom and bath, seeing Glorie's handiwork in every room, before coming back to the living room where she waited with a small, expectant smile on her face.

The little house radiated cleanliness softened with a deep abiding warmth, its ill usage banished or hidden by soap and water, hard work and originality, perhaps even a little love. In its long convoluted history had anyone but Glorie Pellman ever actually loved this place? he wondered. Perhaps that's what was missing all these years and why the house now felt different somehow.

He'd learned today that this woman wasn't what he originally thought her to be. All right, *wanted* her to be, he recognized in a sudden moment of insight. She wasn't Marina; and she wasn't little Mary Sunshine. But she had all the instincts of an earth mother...and she was a nice woman.

Glorie Pellman scared the hell out of him. If he wasn't careful, the need for home and family that had haunted him all his life could center on this woman, just like it once centered on his grandmother, then on his neighbors, and finally on Marina. But he doubted Glorie's leaving would be the relief Marina's had been.

Keeping the golden-eyed witch at arm's length suddenly took on top priority.

Hank's eyes flicked once more around the bright comfortable room before coming to rest on its creator, windblown and sun-touched, who stood looking over her handiwork with understandable pride.

"Nice," he drawled in acknowledgement, his fear pushing him to words guaranteed to drive wedges. "Any man looking for a home won't be able to leave after he sees what you've accomplished with this old barn. When you're ready, you ought to be able to catch you a man in no time at all."

Gloria stepped back, the smile vanishing, leaving her mouth tight and angry. She walked to the front door and held it open pointedly. "Thank you for the lift home."

"No problem. I needed to pick up a part for the Mustang coming in on this afternoon's bus. See you around, Jim." He walked out the front door with his usual cat-footed grace, but feeling mean and not at all as if he'd had the last word.

Gloria closed the door with a restrained bang, wishing with all her heart she'd slammed it hard enough to make the windows rattle, preferably on that...that uncouth mountain man's fingers.

Damn Hank Mason anyway.

Hank heard the door bang behind him, knowing exactly what restraint Glorie had just exercised to

keep from slamming it hard enough to knock it off
its hinges.

He'd been needlessly rude. Hell, he'd been a
horse's behind! The thought shamed him.

The thought angered him.

Climbing into the battered old Mustang, he sighed
in frustration. He owed the woman an apology, dammit. If he'd just kept his mouth shut they'd have been
quits. Now that she'd repaid the money he loaned
her, there should be no more strings, but now he
owed her.

The motor took a little patient coaxing this time
after its good behavior on the mountain, but it turned
over at last and Hank backed the car out of the driveway and pointed it toward the mountain.

What really galled the hell out of him was his brief
moment of dismay when Glorie Pellman repaid the
money and he realized he didn't want it, that he liked
having that tie between them, liked knowing there
was still a reason for them to come in personal contact.

Had he subconsciously tried to reweave the string
by obligating himself with the apology he now owed
her?

Ah, hell. Get a grip, Mason. Thanks to Gloria
whatever-her-name-was-then, you gave up playing
debit and credit games at fifteen. Remember?

His foot angrily punched the accelerator and the
Mustang promptly stalled. Guiding it toward the curb
while it still had motion, Hank took the vehicle out
of the flow of traffic and tried to restart it.

This time, however, the Mustang remained stubbornly powerless. Not until he got out, put the hood
up and fiddled with the engine did it deign to cough
back into life.

Hank sat behind the wheel and let the motor idle for a few minutes, the old sports car now purring as well as it could, and considered his options for what remained of the day. He could go back to the cabin and continue the work on the Mustang Glorie's visit interrupted. Certainly, the little car wasn't feeling all that swift, pardon the pun.

Or he could sit on his front porch and read the paperback he bought yesterday, lean up against the same post where he'd held Jim's sturdy little body on his lap...the spot where the child had listened to his heart.

That picnic lunch had been kind of meager. He could fix an early supper...in the kitchen where he'd kissed Glorie this afternoon. Or he could head back to the cliff...where he'd kissed her again.

A nothing kiss, that one. A sweet touching of mouths. He'd never in his life kissed a woman like that. And with a five-year-old kid as an audience, yet.

So why had his heart knocked against his chest like it was going to leap over the edge of his favorite high spot? And why, when he raised his face from Glorie's and broke the soft contact, did he feel that a piece of him would be forever missing?

Well, he might owe the woman an apology, but that moment of clarity in her living room was right on the money. Glorie Pellman was one dangerous lady.

Hank returned to the cabin, but only to pick up his sleeping bag. After throwing it and a loaf of bread, jar of peanut butter, coffee and coffeepot into the backseat, he headed for the welcome emptiness of the desert. Somewhere Glorie had never been.

Chapter Seven

As usual, Hank and Johnny Holt took their coffee break at Mom's. While Johnny laughed with another of the regulars, Hank managed to tell Gloria casually as she refilled his coffee cup, "Sorry about yesterday's comment. I was out of line."

She didn't even look up but nodded, replying just as casually, "No problem," before moving on down the counter, topping up any empty cups along the way.

Hank could almost hear the snap of the last string. No anger, no zinging response, no scathing looks from golden eyes that carried their own electricity. Just, "No problem."

So why was he feeling mean again?

Abandoning his filled cup, Hank left a bill on the counter and took himself out of Mom's and into the bright Tulaca sunshine. Jim was playing on the swing set. He'd go talk to the boy awhile. The kid's shy quietness had a way of making Hank quiet on the inside, too.

Gloria knew exactly when Hank left. She removed his cup and wiped his spot at the counter so that in seconds it looked as if he'd never been there. Perversely, she wished she could put his cup back again.

The man had apologized. Again. She hadn't received so many apologies since Eric repeatedly begged forgiveness for hurting her.

She didn't have much faith in apologies.

But from Hank? She had the feeling he apologized only after digging the words out with a crowbar, as if he were digging a tall pine out of the ground by the roots. Apologetic words didn't come easy to him and they probably didn't come often. And now he'd forced them out two days in a row.

He didn't *beg* forgiveness, either. Here it is, take it or leave it.

Okay, she'd think about it.

As soon as Jamey saw Hank approach the fence, he jumped off the swing he'd been twining in circles and ran to meet him. The small action caused a fist to wrap itself around Hank's heart and squeeze.

But as the boy approached, his eager run became slow, cautious steps.

"Thought I'd stop by a minute, Jim," Hank said easily, "and see how you're doing."

Jamey put his fingers through the loops in the chain-link fence and leaned his small belly into it. Hank's words made him feel grown up.

"Fine," he replied shyly, then repeated the question he heard the other men ritually ask in greeting one another, even mimicking the lazy Western drawl. "How're you doin'?"

Hank's mouth tilted a bit before he, too, drawled the expected answer. "Can't complain, Jim."

The two stood quietly a few minutes, enjoying each other's company in the shade of the spot they'd chosen, beneath the spreading branches of a cotton-wood growing between the Blackwells' fence and the road.

Jim watched a pickup rattle past and Hank smiled to himself, understanding perfectly the fascination of anything with wheels to a small boy. He'd personally never grown out of it. Watching the kid's golden eyes light up when cars were mentioned was a real kick.

How could anyone want to hurt a kid like Jim? Or a woman like Glorie? She was all hair and eyes and defiance, but still just a slip of a thing. And the boy was little more than a baby now, let alone the toddler he'd been when his father...

Anger roiled in Hank's gut and for a moment he pictured the joy of having Eric Pellman in his face right at that moment. The man had held the world in his hands and he'd hurt them. He'd *hurt* them!

His angry gaze dropped to the boy again and all thought of Eric fled. Jim was looking at him as if he were the devil come to steal the child's soul. Slowly the boy backed away.

Hank wiped a hand over his face. He knew better than to try to coax him back. "It's this ugly mug of mine, Jim," he said conversationally, as if unaware that the child was petrified. "When I think about...um...unpleasant things, my face looks kind'a unpleasant, too." He smiled ruefully when the boy halted. "Not much I can do about it, though. A man's stuck with his face."

Jim drifted back. "I like your face, Hank," he said softly, then added with all the honesty of a five-year-old, "But sometimes it looks scary."

Hank nodded. "Yeah, I know. Looks don't mean much, though. It's what a person does that counts." He paused. "You might want to remember that, son."

Son. The word slipped out faster than thought, leaving a bittersweet taste behind.

Again, the two of them stood in companionable silence. A jet droned by overhead and the distant hum of a semi could be heard from the interstate at the far edge of town.

"My mama says you look like your mountain," Jim said at last.

"Does she?" A mountain, huh? Well, that was one way of describing him. Marina had said much the same thing. She'd called his face a pile of concrete rubble.

"Yes. Mama said mountains are made out of rocks so they will last a long time. She says your mountain is beautiful. That means you're beautiful, too, Hank."

Hank grinned, the humor of being called beautiful lighting up the hard, dark angles of his features. "Hold that thought, Jim," he said.

Glancing out the window to check on Jamey, Gloria saw Hank Mason standing on one side of the Blackwells' fence, apparently talking to her son. He stood, long legs slightly apart and thumbs tucked into the pockets of his jeans in the unconsciously graceful slouch of the outdoor Western male.

On the other side of the fence was Jamey, feet apart, thumbs in his pockets in mirror image.

Tall man, small boy; one all darkness and one all light.

"Gloria? How about a couple of slices of coconut pie for me and Simmons here?"

"Sure thing, Mr. Pollard. Coming right up."

Turning from the window, Gloria hurried behind the counter to get the men their pie. By the time she took it to them, she was composed and smiling.

But she glanced briefly out the window again at the two standing at the edge of the Blackwells' yard.

You're forgiven, Hank Mason, she thought and went after the coffeepot.

Hank avoided Mom's. He told himself he got enough idle talk at the garage; he didn't need it in a restaurant, as well. Talk in Tulaca tended to be repetitive anyway.

It had nothing to do with the fact that Gloria Pellman was haunting his mountain, that he'd spent several more nights in the desert, that he was putting "out of sight, out of mind" to the test.

No, when he went into Tulaca two or three times a week he'd had his meals already, didn't want any coffee, was far too busy.

But he was never too busy to stop and talk to Jim for a few minutes. If Jim's mama's doings were frequently part of the conversation, well, that's just the way kids were. And it was only polite to ask Glorie's son how his mama was doing, wasn't it?

He learned Glorie had dug a garden around the

front steps of five-oh-three Madison and that Jim helped her plant flower seeds. Hank doubted flowers would add much to the old eyesore, but his cynicism couldn't last in the face of Jim's enthusiasm.

His mama bought a new dress, Jim reported. A blue one that made her look real pretty. Didn't Hank think his mama was pretty?

"All mamas are pretty," Hank said shortly. Blue. He knew just how beautiful she'd look in blue. Now just where the hell was Gloria Pellman going to wear her pretty dress?

But Jim had the answer to that unspoken question. "She wore it to church on Sunday," the boy said ingenuously. "Mrs. Reverend Bill thinks my mama's pretty, too. She said so."

"A preacher might get things a little confused now and then, but a preacher's wife is seldom wrong, Jim," Hank said blandly. "You might want to remember that."

And Hank learned that Gloria went to the Snip'n'-Curl to have her hair cut. Something slimy swiggled through his belly.

"About this much," Jim said, and held his thumb and forefinger about an inch apart.

Hank felt himself relax.

"Your face looked kind'a scary again, Hank," Jim said, not frightened this time but curious.

"Indigestion," Hank replied. "You ever been fishing, son?"

Gloria hadn't seen Hank for two weeks, not that she was counting. But she saw the Mustang several times as it passed in front of the café on Tulaca's main street.

A couple of times as she glanced out the window to check on Jamey playing in the Blackwells' shaded lawn she saw the aged sports car parked by the side of the road as its owner talked to Jamey, who leaned excitedly against the chain-link fence.

On one of these occasions Jamey suddenly broke away from the fence and ran toward the rear door of the café that opened on to the back lawn of the Blackwells' home. Something in the way he ran caused Gloria's heart to sink.

She looked hurriedly around the dining room wondering how Sheriff Hazlett and Glen Bigelow, quietly gossiping over cups of coffee and her already famous coconut pie, would react to having their discussion shattered by an upset little boy.

When Jamey came bursting into the dining room, however, there was no trace of tears. Instead his small face glowed with excitement, eyes sparkling and cheeks healthily flushed as he gasped for breath to talk.

Before he could catch his breath, however, Hank walked in the front door and took a stool at the counter, his face its usual cynical mask as Jamey scrambled up on the stool beside him.

Gloria paused, the idea catching her unawares.

Mask?

Jamey, however, gave her no time to speculate. "Hank knows where there's lots of fish, Mom. Can I go fishing with him? Please!"

"*May* I, Jamey," she corrected, stalling for time.

"*May* I, Mom? *Please*."

Mom, not mama. He was growing up so fast. Just over being a baby and already starting kindergarten in the fall. Gloria looked at her son helplessly. He had never been anywhere with anyone but herself before. What if he fell in?

She frowned at Hank as he doctored his coffee. "Can you swim?" she asked anxiously, only to be completely taken aback when he whooped with sudden laughter as did the other two men openly following this exchange.

"Ah, Mom." Jamey ducked his head as if to allow the men's mirth to roll over him, the picture of small boy embarrassment.

Gloria, immediately contrite and cheeks flaming, was still unable to dampen the small flicker of pure enjoyment as she watched Hank Mason laugh again.

"He can swim, ma'am. My fishing boat tipped over in the middle of the lake a few years back and Hank here pulled me out by the hair of my head," Sheriff Hazlett volunteered. "Course, though, I've never been the same since," and he rubbed his balding pate.

"Where you gonna take the boy, Hank?" Glen Bigelow asked when the laughter died down.

"I thought we'd try Three Mile Creek. The water's only up to my waist this time of year so I won't have to swim much if Jim decides to run the fish down instead of using a pole and line."

Jamey looked up from the glass of milk his mother had poured for him and giggled.

Gloria, absently wiping the countertop, stilled, her heart catching. Jamey had giggled, a normal child's infectious unabashed giggle, the sweetest music she'd ever heard! Not daring to raise her eyes, she resumed wiping the counter.

A casual hand reached out and blocked the path

of the frantic cloth bent on scrubbing the pattern off the Formica.

Under cover of the general talk of favorite fishing spots and unforgettable catches, she looked up into black eyes holding a faint questioning. Seen through the sheen of unshed tears, Hank's face didn't look hard at all.

Gloria cleared her throat, her misty gaze swinging toward her son who listened to this man-talk with an air of importance since it now included himself.

"It's…just that he doesn't…giggle like that very often."

Hank's slow smile jellied her heart.

Two clerical aides from the lawyer's office down the street came in and Gloria was at their table, pouring coffee as Hank and Jamey got up to leave.

"I'll have him home before dark," Hank informed her in passing, and left a bill on the cash register.

Gloria, bemused by the look on the younger secretary's face as Hank passed by, forgot she'd not given definite permission for Jamey to go.

Strange that the thought of Hank appealing to other women had not occurred to her. For a moment her eyes narrowed on the frankly admiring look in the secretary's eyes.

Well, she supposed some might be attracted to his lean hard-bitten appearance. "Hank looks like his mountain," she'd once told Jamey. And though not really handsome, when Hank Mason smiled, he was the sexiest man alive.

If a woman was interested in his type, of course.

"How's the husband and kids?" she asked the secretary casually.

Gloria kept one eye out the wide front windows all afternoon until preparation for the evening meal had her too busy to worry.

By eight, however, when it was time to go home and Hank and Jamey still hadn't returned, she was in a panic. Yet it was still light and would be until after nine o'clock on the long summer evenings.

Only this fact kept her from calling the sheriff and filing a missing person report.

She made the short walk home with her stomach in knots. How could she have been so thoughtless? For all she knew, Three Mile Creek was in another state. Why hadn't she asked? Why hadn't she made Hank give her a definite time, instead of accepting his nebulous "by dark"?

Did he mean dark dark, or dusk? When the sun set, or when the stars came out?

Her thoughts trailed away as she rounded the corner to see the battered Mustang parked in her drive. Letting out a shuddering breath of relief, she immediately huffed the breath back in again in irritation. By the time she was near enough to the house to see Hank and Jamey sitting placidly on the front steps, she'd worked herself into a fine rage.

"You said you'd bring him back, Hank Mason! How was I supposed to know you were home? Didn't you realize I'd be nearly out of my mind with worry? Is this the way you... Oh!"

Jamey left the porch and ran toward her, covered hair to sneakers with mud, an excited grin splitting his face.

"I caught two fishes, Mama, all by myself! Hank just helped me take the hook out. Come see! They're in the ice chest. Hank caught some, too. We—"

"James Allen Pellman, look at you! That shirt will never come clean. And your arm is bleeding. What has Hank done to you? I never…"

She never knew when Hank left the front porch but he stood suddenly beside her, holding her upper arm just tight enough for her to recognize the steel in his grip. "That's enough, Glorie."

His quietly spoken words checked her, but only long enough for her to refocus her wrath.

"And you! You could both have been drowned and I wouldn't even have known where—"

He kissed her, the merest touch on her mouth, but containing an unmistakable message. It silenced her completely as she gazed into the warning face just above her own.

Her gaze, following his, dropped to her son.

All she could see was the back half of Jamey's fair head, but as she watched, a drop of moisture plopped onto the toe of one already wet and muddied sneaker.

Without thinking, Gloria sat on the cracked sidewalk leading to the front porch and took the boy into her lap. His back remained resentfully stiff and straight, however, and he refused to look at her, forcing her to put her hand under his chin and tilt his face toward her own.

Her breath caught.

For the first time in his life she saw in Jamey's eyes what others often saw in her own. Golden flecks ignited into small fires seemed to shoot sparks straight at her. Tears made muddy rivulets down his dirty face all right, but from the tips of his hair sticking up in spikes to his slime-encrusted tennis shoes, Jamey was angry.

Somewhere in the muddy bottom of Three Mile Creek, and hopefully gone forever, was her son's unnaturally quiet acceptance of all that came his way. The child's hostile eyes fixed themselves on his mother.

"Hank didn't do nothin' to me. I scratched myself on a bush. And ever'body gets dirty when they slip in the mud. It's one of the hazards of fishing, Hank said."

His voice held all the considerable dignity a young boy can possess, and Gloria dropped her lashes, afraid her eyes would show the joy suddenly bubbling inside her.

She swallowed and took a deep breath to keep her voice even. "I'm sorry, honey." She really was, and ashamed of ruining Jamey's pleasure in his first fishing trip. "I was worried and I allowed my worry to make me angry. Silly, I know, but I hope you and Hank will forgive me."

"Hank and me can take care of ourselves. You don't have to worry." The anger faded from the golden brown eyes but her son's tone still held a hint of rebuff.

Gloria gave a small laugh as she lifted him off her lap, not daring to kiss him.

"When you love someone, sweetie, you often worry even when it's not needed. Now show me your fish." She went to scramble off the sidewalk but found Hank's hand in front of her, ready to give assistance.

She used it to lever herself up but the man's look of dry amusement put her back up so that she snapped, "You could have called or stopped by the café. I had you both pictured at the bottom of the river. Surely *you* realized I'd worry about you."

A glacial chill instantly replaced the amusement. "Your concern is your problem, Gloria. Keep me out of it."

She opened her mouth, ready to tear into him, only to close it again slowly. He'd called her Gloria.

What had she said to drive him so far away? Only that she worried about him.

Her eyes widened slightly in surprise as, unconsciously, she searched the planes and angles of his face.

How he would hate knowing that, this man who treasured his aloneness above all things. Hank Mason was a giving man, would give anybody anything, as she should know. But above all things, he hated receiving.

And she, a pride-filled woman herself, was dishing out concern as if it were charity at Christmastime, then expecting him to be grateful. Yet she could no more not worry about him than she could not worry about Jamey.

Her hand reached out to touch him, but she drew it back again, her face unknowingly wistful.

"See my fish, Mama."

Jamey stood proudly beside the plastic ice chest, holding it open with one hand. Gloria hurried forward to look, glad to at least be back in her son's good graces.

"We cleaned them in the backyard and got the bones out while we waited for you to come home. They just need to be cooked, Hank said. He said he'd show you how."

Gloria admired the catch with proper enthusiasm.

She wasn't sure how she felt about all the "Hank saids", however. For such a silent man, Hank seemed to have said quite a bit.

As if reading her mind, Hank reached out and ruffled Jamey's mud-stiffened hair. "We'll save eating them for another time, Jim. They'll keep in the freezer. Your mother has been cooking all day and is tired now."

Jamey looked stricken. "But you said…" he began, only to be silenced by something in Hank's gaze. The small grubby face fell but he swallowed manfully. "Yes, sir." The words a soft, defeated whisper.

His mother, however, feeling she'd done enough damage for one day, turned the full battery of her own aristocratic bearing on the hard-faced man standing beside her.

Hank smiled inwardly at the pride and inflexible honor in the flared nostrils of Glorie's small defined nose, but her eyes carried gold-etched guile.

Now what was the woman up to?

Gloria Pellman had a way of pushing his buttons as if she didn't give a damn what explosions she might set off…and he could never guess which button she was going to push next. In fact, he always seemed to be holding his breath around her.

"But Hank said," she repeated Jamey's words with soft insinuation, giving velvet emphasis to the word *said,* daring him to go back on his word to a child. There were some who would, but not Hank Mason, and they both knew it.

Admiration for her maneuver touched his features, gone in an instant as he raked a hand through his hair. The gesture left a black strand falling across his forehead, softening the rough contours of his face.

He took a deep breath, knowing it wasn't one of his better decisions and wondering if he'd survive the next couple of hours unscathed, but he bent to pick up the ice chest by its two side handles.

"I warn you I'm not in the best of moods," he said. "I hope you know what you're doing."

Gloria merely wrinkled her nose at him. "I know, all right," she said as she unlocked the front door. "Just follow my lead."

Hank chuckled to himself, but carried the chest through to the kitchen and put it on the floor near the sink. For a nice woman, Glorie wasn't too bad— as long as she didn't try to take care of him. Her concern made him nervous. She ought to save it for her kid.

Surveying Jamey, Gloria suddenly grinned. "I think you'd better have your bath before dinner tonight, kiddo. Otherwise I might think we've been invaded by—" her voice dropped to a dramatic whisper "—the Creature From Three Mile Creek."

He giggled and her heart danced. Would she ever get used to the magic of that sound?

But in normal tones she added, "Get your pajamas and I'll meet you in the bathroom."

"Can't Hank give me my bath tonight?"

"Now, Jamey—"

"Aren't you old enough to bathe yourself, Jim?" Hank asked curiously.

Jamey flushed to the roots of his hair.

"Fix the water, I mean," the boy mumbled, finding the floor of extreme interest.

He had never been allowed to bathe himself and

Gloria frowned, wondering for the first time if she was holding Jamey back, keeping him dependent on her unwittingly. She was intelligent enough to know if that was the case, his first year in school would be a nightmare.

Mother and son were both grateful when Hank said easily, "Sure, I'll fix the water for you, Jim. How do you want it? Steamy, tepid, or ice cold?"

"Tepid."

Gloria could almost see Jamey rolling the new word around in his mind.

When he tacked on, "What's that mean?" Hank chuckled and launched into an explanation that carried the boy toward the bathroom.

Gloria had dinner well under control when Hank came back into the kitchen, splashing noises coming from behind him. He frowned when he saw her dredging the fish in cornmeal as she waited for the oil in the big iron skillet on the stove to get hot enough for quick frying.

"I was going to do that, Glorie. You really must be tired."

"Never too tired to cook my son's first fish. This is a dinner I'll enjoy preparing. And," she added mischievously, "I'm a better cook than you."

His mouth quirked in acknowledgement. "Well, there's no way I can ruin potatoes if all I do is peel them." He picked up the potato peeler and began scraping the potatoes she had taken out in readiness.

They worked together in silence for a few minutes before Gloria said musingly, "It's been a day of firsts for Jamey. First fish, first giggle, first time to really show anger."

"First time the chick left his place under his mama's wing,'' Hank said, then smiled to himself thinking of Gloria's reaction when she'd seen her only son frosted with mud. He wanted to laugh aloud at the memory of her horrified face but didn't quite dare. She probably didn't think it so funny.

Unaware, and her eyes watching her hands as they continued to work, Gloria stood silently a moment, but when she looked up, her gaze was candidly direct.

"First time to bathe himself," she added flatly, determined to be honest. "I've been overprotective, haven't I?"

Hank's humor fled. Why the hell was she asking *him* a question like that? How was he supposed to know? He lifted a hand before realizing it held the potato peeler.

Gloria smiled as he looked at his raised hand blankly, knowing instinctively that he had wanted to push it through his hair.

But he returned to slowly peeling the potatoes as he sought for words, both flattered and chagrined that this woman had turned to him with her concern. Yet what kind of advice could a man with his background give?

The hell of it was, there were men in the world born to be husbands and fathers, who knew to a nicety how families were supposed to function. One of them was probably just waiting to find Glorie and Jim. Or for the two of them to find him. And when they did, he'd be the world's luckiest man.

"I'm not the person to ask, Glorie," Hank said at last. "You know I don't know anything about kids and my own childhood certainly wasn't anything to use as an example. I grew up bathing myself from the earliest I can remember, but I also bathed only when I pleased. In fact, I always did exactly as I pleased because my grandmother didn't give a damn what my sister and I did as long as we stayed outside and didn't mess up this iceberg of a house.''

His voice was low and bitter as his black gaze swept over the chintz curtains at the kitchen windows, the plants massed in a corner, the colorful photographs from old magazines that Gloria had taped to the dingy cabinet doors in an effort to conceal their need of paint she couldn't yet afford.

Her eyes widened as she took in the implication of his words. ''*This* was your home?'' she finally asked, and flinched at the derisive laugh he gave in answer.

''No, this wasn't my home. It was a house I lived in whenever the weather was bad and I couldn't find anywhere else to go. The streets of Tulaca and the mountain were more a home than this pile of lumber. Cleanliness was godliness in my grandmother's view and she kept this house so clean everyone was afraid to walk in it. My first fish rotted in the garbage heap because she wouldn't allow it in the door.''

Gloria kept her back to him as she fried the fish at the stove, sensing he wasn't really aware of what his bitterness toward the house revealed.

Picking up the paring knife, Hank sliced the potatoes for fries with a precision bordering on viciousness, his mind obviously on his childhood.

''It might have been clean, but this house was only a cold, cheerless barn to me. Nothing in it reflected warmth. They say the way a woman keeps her house is a reflection of her personality. It must be true because my grandmother kept herself as she kept the house, clean and cheerless. I don't remember her ever sweating or ever smiling.''

Silently Gloria took the sliced potatoes from in front of him and substituted a head of lettuce that Hank immediately began chopping for a salad.

"And your mother?" she asked matter-of-factly, still not looking at him. Tears threatened but she swallowed them back, knowing that if Hank had even an inkling of her feelings this would be the last time either she or Jamey saw him.

And the thought of this silent, lonely man walking out of her life forever was somehow unbearable. The potatoes sizzled and bubbled as she eased them into the hot oil.

"She took off as soon as Anna was born. I used to hate her for not marrying and giving us a real home, but after going through the hell of a marriage myself, I can understand why it had no appeal for her. I just never understood why she couldn't have taken us with her."

Something in the quality of the ensuing silence compelled Gloria to turn and look at him.

He stared at her, his eyes flat with a hostility that left a burning coldness deep in her heart.

"It was a horrible childhood and Anna was better out of it, but there's no reason for anyone to pity me. I learned a lesson then that some spend a lifetime trying to learn—one that hurts a hell of a lot less when you're young. If you can't stand on your own two feet and spit in the eye of what hurts you, then you're better off dead. Needing someone's shoulder to cry on is the most useless emotion there is."

Gloria could only stare back at him silently. Instinct fought his words, but experience had taught her the same lesson. The kitchen seemed to lose some of the charm so painstakingly applied to its surface and her eyes swung to a greasy spot on the far wall that had somehow remained uncovered.

"Yes," she answered at last, "I know."

Hank went back to chopping tomatoes, hating the pain his words had etched in Glorie's eyes. His tough little Glorie was so damn vulnerable.

Don't listen to me, he wanted to say. Sometimes people do need a shoulder to cry on. At three o'clock one morning you were there for me, the way no one in my life ever was.

But the words wouldn't come.

His knife cleaved into another tomato, halving it, quartering.

It's the needing someone, he wanted to say, that keeps a man awake nights; that at unexpected moments has him thinking of mothers and fathers and three point two children. It's need that causes a man to trade pride for empty dreams.

But the words remained caught in ancient rusted chains, prisoners deep in his gut where there was no light.

Another tomato, halved, quartered.

And, Glorie, he wanted to warn, don't try to give to me. For why would you, except from pity? Your stubborn pride has left me nothing to trade.

Worse, when you're near I lose all control and kissing you becomes an obsession. Yet to kiss you throws my body into such sexual shock that it's all I can do to keep from hauling you off to the nearest flat surface. And I can't seem to control that, either.

Hank looked up at Gloria, standing at the stove with her small straight back to him, her hair a wild, uncontained mass rippling past her shoulders.

Words strained, but the old chains held.

Chapter Eight

Mop in hand, Gloria surveyed her still damp kitchen floor and sighed. Cleaning, scrubbing, waxing...nothing would save this old linoleum but covering it over with new.

"Might as well shoot it, Glorie. It's done for."

Startled, she turned to find Hank just behind her.

"Jim let me in," he said. "Guess with the radio going, you didn't hear me knock."

She laughed and walked over to turn down the station playing classic rock and roll. "Music to mop by," she quipped. "What brings you off the mountain this morning? I thought Johnny closed his garage on Saturdays."

"He does. I wanted to talk to you."

"Oh? How about doing it over coffee, if you have time? I'm ready for a break."

"I have time." He widened his finely shaped nostrils. "That's not just floor cleaner I smell." Glorie's laugh tickled once more through his senses.

"Oatmeal cookies, Sherlock. I think I can probably find a couple for you."

Hank mentally backed up a step, suddenly not liking the sound of this little by-play. "I wasn't—"

"Are you ready for a milk break, Jamey?" Gloria interrupted, not realizing he'd been about to speak.

Jamey left his trucks on their superhighway of blocks. "With cookies?"

Gloria winked at Hank, surprising him into a smile. "With cookies."

In Tulaca's high desert environment, the kitchen floor had dried in minutes and Gloria busied herself putting the coffee on, then taking down cups and a glass for Jamey. Finally she selected cookies from the cooling racks on the counter and arranged them on a plate.

Gloria had just put the plate on the table and was turning away when one of Jamey's hands crept out. Immediately she whirled back again and slapped the boy's hand lightly. "Gotcha," she said triumphantly.

But her triumph was short-lived, for without her even being aware of when he'd taken it, Hank held up a cookie.

Jamey giggled.

Slowly, ostentatiously, Hank broke the cookie in two equal pieces, handing Jamey one of them and popping the other into his own mouth, his eyes, full of dark merriment, never leaving Gloria's face.

Gloria put her hands on her hips. "Why you slick so-and-so."

She looked from the man to Jamey, who also slowly chewed his cookie without taking his eyes off his mother's face, mischief in every line of his small body.

"I can tell I'm going to have to stay on the alert around the two of you," Gloria said huffily. "But don't think you're getting away with anything. This just means you each get one less." With an ostentation the equal of Hank's, she took two cookies off the plate and put them back on the wire racks.

Hank and Jamey looked at each other and grimaced. However, since the plate was heaped with a child's hand-size cookies, they probably wouldn't starve.

As Gloria poured coffee into his cup, Hank asked curiously, "How do you cook all week at Mom's and then have any desire to bake on a Saturday? Seems like you'd be sick of kitchens."

She laughed.

Glorie, Hank was beginning to learn, was a laughing kind of woman.

"Easy," she said. "I cook to relax, just like you work on cars."

Now how had she known that? Hank wondered as he took a bite on the side of the cookie that held the most raisins.

When Jamey left the table to go back to his trucks, Gloria poured Hank and herself another cup of coffee, one ear tuned to the low "v-rooooms" and "beeps" coming from the next room. Like many only children, Jamey slipped easily into a world of his own.

There were no children his age for him to play with in this neighborhood and Gloria had little opportunity to meet and socialize with other young mothers. His lack of playmates worried her. Would

Jamey have difficulty relating to others of his age when he started school?

"He plays well by himself, doesn't he?" Hank said quietly, reading her thoughts.

"Yes. I suppose I'm fortunate. Jamey never gets bored."

She absently gathered stray crumbs with an index finger. It seemed natural to voice her worries aloud to Hank. "I'm anxious about him starting school, though, and being able to get along with other children."

Uncharacteristically, Hank cleared his throat and used the handle to rock his cup back and forth, watching it warily as if it were a bomb about to explode in his face. "Well...uh...that's what I wanted to talk to you about, Glorie."

When she didn't answer, he continued doggedly, still not looking at her. "What I mean is, I wondered if you might like to go with me to visit the Flannigans next weekend."

Gloria frowned. "The Flannigans?"

"They're friends of mine." For the first time since beginning the conversation, Hank looked up. "Joaquin especially. He and his wife live on a ranch the other side of Albuquerque, and have three kids."

When Gloria's face remained blank, Hank elaborated. "The kids aren't exactly Jim's age, but close enough to give him someone to play with, I suppose. And Jane knows all about raising kids. She's a good mother."

Jane. The name, dropping so easily from Hank's lips, reached out and slapped Gloria in the face.

"Oh?" she said inanely.

She must have sounded doubtful because Hank frowned.

"Well, she must be," he said tersely. "Her kids are healthy, polite without being subservient, and seem intelligent enough."

And what is my kid, Gloria thought with a tinge of jealousy, a sickly, ignorant, juvenile delinquent? "Thank you for inviting me," she began stiffly, "but I don't..."

"You might at least give it some consideration." Hank's voice roughened with nervous irritability. "You're the one who asked for advice on seeing to it Jim grows into a well-adjusted youngster. I can't give it to you, but someone like Jane, with her experience, can. With Jane and Joaquin you'll get a chance to see how children act in a normal household."

Gloria was quiet a moment, sure she wouldn't like Jane the Paragon at all. "The other side of Albuquerque? That's a long way," she said slowly.

"We'd have to spend the night, yes. But the house is huge. A true Spanish hacienda, in fact."

"Won't your friends object to you bringing people they don't know into their home?"

Hank grinned, relaxed now that he knew he was getting his own way. "Jane loves company. So does Joaquin, for that matter. I'll pick you up next Saturday morning around five."

"Five?" Gloria's voice was faint.

"Five."

He stood and, to the surprise of both of them, leaned over and kissed her lightly on the cheek. Then he went into the living room to say goodbye to Jim.

Before he left, however, Gloria came in to give

him a covered plastic container full of oatmeal cookies.

But I haven't given *you* anything, he thought hazily, and felt like a man with his car stalled on the railroad tracks who suddenly hears a train whistle. Disaster hurtled toward him and there wasn't a damn thing he could do about it.

Gloria thrust the container into his hands before his defensive sarcasm could fill the breach, however.

"These are for Charley," she said. "But maybe he'll share."

When he left, Hank carried the container of cookies in his large mechanic's hands as if it were a ticking bomb, knowing himself well and truly routed.

A plume of reddish brown dust billowed behind the Mustang as it turned off the paved highway onto the dirt ranch road. Except for the few heads of cattle seen occasionally, the land baked empty and treeless in the summer heat.

"Tired?"

Hank sat easily behind the wheel, keeping the car on the road with his left hand, his elbow propped on the window frame. His other hand lay on his lap, the last two fingers bandaged onto a metal brace.

"A little. How's the hand?"

"Stiff." His mouth tightened imperceptibly. Damn fool thing to do. Just went to show what thinking of a woman could do to a man.

Yesterday Johnny Holt had made some teasing comment on the luscious length of Gloria's legs and Hank's quick anger had cost him his concentration just as he delicately maneuvered an engine into position as it was being lowered by a winch. Distracted by his irritation, he hadn't taken his hand away soon enough as the engine settled into place. Two fingers were broken. The pain niggling at him now was nothing to the agony he had suffered during the couple of minutes it had taken Johnny to lift the heavy engine off the side of his hand.

Gloria had known nothing of the accident until this morning around dawn when he'd come to pick up her and the boy. Then she'd looked from his hand to his face where he'd stood on the front steps in the half light of the early hour.

"What happened?" she'd asked quietly.

"Caught my hand under a motor. Are you ready?"

She hadn't answered and she hadn't moved. "And?" she'd asked instead.

"And what?"

Hank knew he'd sounded belligerent, but he didn't care. Not the way he was feeling.

"What kind of damage did you do to your hand, Hank?" Gloria's tone was patient.

"Two broken fingers and some muscle bruising. Give me your bags, Glorie, and hustle up Jim so we can get on the road. We have a long way to go."

"No. You can use my phone to call the Flannigans and tell them we're not coming this weekend."

Immediately he stiffened, not liking her tone of voice. Her *caring* tone of voice. "Glorie…"

"I mean it, Hank. Broken fingers may not seem like much, but I know it is. You're in pain and you're tired and you have no business making a long trip this weekend. Give your hand a chance to rest."

From her position in the doorway, her face on a level with his, he could see her usually soft mouth drawn into a tight line of determination every bit as stubborn as his own. Her hair in braids and looped into a coronet around her head only added to her Aztec princess look.

It took considerable willpower and as much mockery as he could muster not to kiss her—and to get her fanny finally into the car.

"Are you trying to mother me?" he asked silkily.

Her anger flared at once as he'd known it would. "Look, Hank…"

"No, you look, Glorie. I'm going to the Flannigans' with or without you, so make up your mind what you're going to do. If the hand gives me too much trouble I'll take one of the pain pills the doc prescribed."

She'd opened her mouth, but at his last words closed it again, her gaze narrowing. "When did you last take one?"

He realized at once he'd just made a tactical error. "I haven't yet," he'd admitted, "but I will if I need it."

"Now," Gloria had said, and he'd taken the damned pill.

They hadn't been on the road an hour when the medication began to show its strength. Again, Glorie seemed to sense the narcotic effect it had on his body almost before he did.

"Let me drive awhile, Hank, while you rest."

The offer was made without undue sympathy and he recognized the wisdom of the suggestion, pulling over to the side of the road so they could switch places. For some reason he'd not doubted Glorie's ability to handle the Mustang, now truly named after his specialized work on it. Lord knows she could handle anything else.

"This highway will take you to Albuquerque," he directed. "But then the way gets tricky. We won't be in Albuquerque for at least another three hours, however, and I'll be awake long before that."

He watched as she accelerated off the side of the road and onto the highway. Sure enough, Gloria used the four-geared stick shift with a smoothness equaling his own. Putting his head back against the bucket seat, he slept.

He'd been mistaken. His sleep deep and dreamless, he hadn't wakened until Glorie gently shook his shoulder. They were in the parking lot of a roadside café frequented by truckers on the outlying fringes of Albuquerque.

Several drivers called to him when the three of them walked into the restaurant for coffee and he hadn't missed the appreciative male glances directed at Glorie. For a moment it was a toss-up as to feeling proud or punching somebody out, and the confusion of his thoughts frazzled his temper, never very stable anyway when he was in the vicinity of this woman.

Naturally they'd been placed in the farthest reaches of the huge restaurant.

"I suppose you know every man in here watched you walk through the place," he commented after they were finally seated and the coffee arrived.

She didn't even lift her head from perusing the menu. "Are my jeans ripped?"

"They're too damn tight."

Then she lifted her head...and her chin. He suddenly wanted to laugh.

"My jeans are no tighter than yours," she replied dangerously. "Tell you what. When you loosen your jeans, I'll loosen mine.'' She clamped her mouth shut suddenly as delicious color ran into her cheeks.

Hank kept his face just bland enough to infuriate her and picked up his own menu. ''It's a deal,'' he said, studying the breakfast list as if his life depended on it.

The menu was plucked from his loose hold so that tigress eyes could glare into his. ''That wasn't what I meant.''

''It wasn't? You mean you don't want us buying jeans together?'' he asked innocently. ''Well, I suppose something like that *could* ruin a woman's reputation.''

Yep. There went her chin again. But the waitress appeared to take their order so he had to wait for her retaliation. She threw it at him just as soon as the waitress left.

''You really are behind the times, Hank,'' Glorie said with all the appearance of pitying sympathy. ''You ought to get off your mountain more often. Reputations are neither made nor broken on the basis of such things anymore, even in small towns like Tulaca. Besides, *your* impeccable reputation should take care of the question of my virtue.''

''I hope you're not basing that assumption on woman's intuition,'' he drawled.

''Ah, but this woman's intuition says you haven't much use for women. You seem remarkably self-sufficient.''

His mouth curved. ''I'll concede women have their uses. The world would be an empty place without 'em. And what with makeup and tight jeans and all, most are mighty decorative.''

Gloria's brows shot up in simulated surprise.

"Recreation and procreation, hmm? Now that's interesting. Since we no longer need their muscle, women have been saying the same about men for years. Do you suppose civilization has reached sexual equality at last?"

He'd chuckled at that.

She was quick, his Glorie, and he loved their verbal matches. Best of all, she always sparred fairly, never hitting below the belt or turning a confidence against him. Judging from her sparkling eyes and the faint flush washing her high cheekbones, she enjoyed their sparring as much as he did.

The boy silently sucked the straw in his orange juice, his big eyes going back and forth between them, following the conversation like a tennis match.

Glorie glanced at her son, caught Hank's eye, and they laughed softly together.

But, after they finished their breakfast and stood to leave the table, he'd courteously held back for Glorie and Jim to precede him when Glorie balked.

"You go first," she told him brazenly. "This time I want to watch *your* tight jeans. It's my turn to see what the women were looking at when we came in."

Her eyes dared him…and damned if he didn't walk in front of her, putting a little extra swagger into it because he hadn't a doubt in the world Glorie's gaze would be right where she said it would be.

As they left the restaurant it seemed only natural to hook an elbow around her neck as they walked. The three of them were laughing together anyway; Jim because he and Glorie were.

"I never knew you were such a show-off," Glorie told him, digging her elbow gently into his rib cage.

He swung her around to face him and their laughter died, but not their smiles.

Jim looked up at them expectantly, his golden eyes bright with curiosity, and a couple of truckers going into the restaurant passed them on the sidewalk. One of the truckers made a comment and the two men laughed.

Hank didn't know what the comment was, but it broke the mood. Glorie blinked and stepped away from him to bend down and tie Jim's sneaker. "It's loose," she told the boy, who stared at his mother's bent head in surprise.

As he drove over the hard-packed dirt road, Hank wondered what Jane, with her clear, all-seeing gray eyes that made a man want to hide or confess his most unmentionable sins, would think of Glorie.

Probably, with her usual accuracy, she'd put two and two together and come up with twenty-two.

Well, they'd reached the Flannigan ranch. Too late to do anything about it now. Did it matter what Jane thought?

Not one damn bit.

Gloria watched with trepidation as the imposing hacienda-style ranch house came into view. Of earth-colored adobe and with no attempt at a formal lawn, it seemed a part of the stark, surrounding landscape, except for several cottonwood trees softening its lines and protecting it from the desert sun.

Hank parked the car in the shade of one of them. Gloria had a swift impression of a large garage with the cab portion of an eighteen-wheeled truck parked in front of it before a flurry of children and dogs came hurtling from the side veranda of the house.

The excited group stopped short at the sight of Jamey being plucked from the backseat by Hank's capable hands. He put the boy down beside him and the children, all immediately tongue-tied, stared silently at each other until a woman erupted in their midst and threw herself into Hank's arms.

"Oh, how I've missed you!" was all Gloria heard, her attention painfully caught by the tender smile spreading over Hank's face as he held the woman tightly in his arms.

He *did* love her!

But when the woman stepped away from Hank and turned to her, Gloria's thoughts stopped abruptly. She found herself being surveyed by a pair of the purest, clearest gray eyes she'd ever seen.

"You're Glorie," the woman said, smiling and holding out a hand, not to shake but to take one of Gloria's into her own. "I'm Jane Flannigan. Welcome to our home." There was no mistaking the sincerity of the welcome. "This smelly bum is my husband, Joaquin."

The "smelly bum" who had now joined them merely grinned, gave his hands a final wipe with a grease-stained rag before stuffing it in the hip pocket of his jumpsuit, and put out a large paw into which Gloria's disappeared.

This time the eyes surveying her were a deep rich blue, a breathtaking contrast to thick black hair and lashes. His obvious Spanish-Irish ancestry had certainly been generous to him in the looks department, Gloria thought.

"I'd like you to meet my son Jamey," she said, and Joaquin gravely shook the boy's hand. Then Jane did, also, smiling gently. Jamey gave her a shy smile in response.

"These brats are anxious to meet you, too, Jamey," Jane said of her own children now clustered around her. "They've been waiting since early this morning for you to get here."

She named them off one by one, with a hand on a head or a shoulder. "Janet Ruth, who is seven and has the unfortunate nickname of Dreamer, which she is."

A knobby-kneed urchin with blue-gray eyes and a mane of tawny hair tied in an off-center ponytail smiled in a slow, sweet, gap-toothed smile.

"Austin Henry, who is six, and known to all and sundry as Audie, except in school where he goes by his much more dignified rightful name."

"Hi, Jamey." Audie was remarkable in that he had a head of thick, curling auburn hair, his father's blue eyes and a generous sprinkling of freckles across his nose.

"My name's Jim," he was told unsmilingly.

Audie looked pleased. "Sure, Jim." His sympathetic grin spoke volumes about knowing just how grown-ups could make life difficult for small boys.

"And the plastic-strip queen here is Maria Elena," Jane concluded just as a small limpet with plasters on both knees and an elbow fastened herself around Jamey's midsection.

Jamey turned a bright beet red and looked around frantically, but Audie came to his rescue.

"Cut it out, Mari," he said briskly, giving the diminutive name its Spanish pronunciation and prying the short, plump arms from around Jamey's waist.

"Don't pay any attention to her, Jim. She hugs ev-er'body. Mari, let *go!*"

The little girl reluctantly dropped her arms only to regard Jamey with huge worshipful brown eyes.

"Wimmin!" pronounced her big brother in disgust. "C'mon, Jim. I'll show you our pups."

Jamey looked at Gloria, who nodded, and ran off with Audie, glancing over his shoulder to make sure the adoring Maria Elena remained behind. Jane, how-ever, took her small daughter firmly by the hand be-fore she could follow. "You and I will show Gloria to her room," she said gently, and Maria Elena, dis-tracted, looked up at Gloria and smiled, the smile transforming her plain little face into a thing of beauty.

Hank went off with Joaquin after carrying her bag to a guest room and Gloria and Jane sat in one shaded corner of the Spanish-style inner courtyard bounded on three sides by the house and on the fourth with an adobe wall. Flowering plants bloomed everywhere and in the center a three-tiered fountain splashed. Gloria caught the flash of goldfish in its lower pond. Birds flitted throughout the trees and a parrot squawked raucously in a large wrought-iron cage hanging from one of the exposed log beams of the porch.

"You have a lovely home," she said apprecia-tively, sitting back in a rattan patio chair and taking a sip of her lemonade. This small oasis of peace and shade did much to dispel her shyness at being in the home of strangers.

Jane smiled wryly. "I suppose I should say thank you, but I can't take credit for its loveliness. The house has been in Joaquin's family since the late seventeen hundreds when this area of the United States belonged to Spain. Even the furnishings are too sturdy and too right for the house for me to change. I had to put the lovely Queen Anne pieces I inherited from my grandmother into storage.''

She laughed. ''It can be frustrating for a new bride to be unable to create a home for her husband in her own style, but I made up for it. Instead of buying furniture and changing the decor, I had children. That seemed the only way I could stamp my personality onto this house. Let's face it. I'm a long way from Elison, Texas.''

Gloria smiled delightedly. ''And I'm a long way from Houston, a mere hundred miles from Elison. Hi, neighbor.''

''Really? I knew as soon as I met you that you were special, but I thought it was because Hank likes you. He doesn't like many women, you know. But of course, if you're from *Texas…*''

They both laughed. ''That has to be it,'' Gloria agreed. ''But actually, Hank just tolerates me. He only brought me along so I could pick up pointers on mothering from you.'' She knew she was fishing even as the words left her mouth.

''You've *got* to be kidding,'' Jane exclaimed incredulously, sitting forward to stare wide-eyed at Gloria. ''What makes him think I'm an authority? I read lots of books, stay awake nights worrying about whether I've warped one of the kids for life, and call my mother once a week. Hank thinks you need pointers from *me?*''

Gloria laughed. ''You're making me feel better already. Actually, Hank just thought I might like a firsthand view of how another woman copes, since I haven't been in Tulaca long enough to know anyone with young children and I lost both my parents several years ago.''

She paused and drew a wet circle with the sweating bottom of her glass on the fringed plastic cloth covering the patio table. "Hank took Jamey fishing a couple of weeks ago," she explained, "and when they weren't back when I thought they should be, I'm afraid I overreacted—" she smiled ruefully "—loudly."

"And Hank blew his top," Jane concluded.

Gloria raised startled eyes. "Oh, no. Actually, he was nicer about it than I deserved. I was really quite silly. But it started me worrying about being overprotective. With Jamey an only child, I don't want to turn him into a sissy or set him up for teasing by the other children once he starts school. I tried asking Hank how much freedom and responsibility he thought Jamey should have for his age, but he told me about his terrible childhood and insisted he wasn't the one to ask, either."

"My God," Jane breathed reverently, awe filling her wide gray eyes. "Let me get this straight," she said, and ticked off the points on her fingers. "Hank took Jamey fishing. You yelled at Hank and are still around to tell the story. You asked Hank's advice on raising children. Hank told you about his childhood in Tulaca. And you believe Hank doesn't think you're special!"

She examined Gloria's puzzled face. "No, I can see you don't. I'll put it this way. First of all, Hank doesn't usually associate with quote, unquote, nice women. He once told me nice women hide their true selves under a protective coating of gentility that makes them worse than the un-nice ones who have the saving grace of being honest in what they are. And secondly, I don't believe anyone, not even Joaquin, knows about Hank's childhood.''

Only the tinkle of the ice in Gloria's glass as she took a sip of lemonade, trying to get her errant thoughts together, broke the following silence. Jane made it sound as if she *were* something special to Hank.

A small spiral of joy feathered deep inside her, only to be overridden by doubt.

She had seen the look on his face when he greeted Jane.

''Hank didn't exactly confide in me,'' she said at last. ''It was a conversation that came about because of my insecurities over Jamey. It's my son Hank looks out for. Jamey thinks he's the most wonderful person in the world, and Hank probably enjoys being worshiped.''

When she looked up, Jane wore a small troubled frown.

''Surely you don't mean that,'' the older woman said gently. ''For one thing, there isn't much to do on a pedestal and Hank is an active man. I can only speak from one point of view, of course, but I know that all Joaquin wants from me and his children is love and respect. Don't you think that might be all Hank wants, too?''

Painful color stained Gloria's face as Jane's softly spoken words hung in the silence. How pompously radical she must have sounded. Yet she didn't hate men, at least not anymore. Not since she'd sat with Hank by the cliff on the mountain. She just couldn't trust them, as Hank couldn't trust women. They were two of a kind.

Her thoughts stopped. Two of a kind, and both so very, very foolish.

Hank must know that all women were not like his first wife or his grandmother. The way they struck sparks off each other, he probably had his doubts about Gloria, but surely Jane was an example of a trustworthy woman. And neither were all men like Eric. Hank, for all his volatile temper, would never hit anyone weaker or smaller than himself, nor would he tolerate such behavior in others.

"I'm sorry, Glorie, I didn't mean to offend you." Jane sat looking at her anxiously and Gloria brought herself back and smiled, covering the other woman's hand with her own.

"I'm the one to apologize," she said. "Hank has been a good friend to Jamey and has asked nothing in return."

She lowered her eyes a moment to study the splash of color in a large flower on the plastic tablecloth, then raised them again to meet the clear, gray, penetrating gaze of the woman across from her. A small rueful smile touched her mouth. "I'm afraid trust isn't easy for me, either, but I'm learning."

And Hank has been my teacher, she thought, recognizing it at last.

Jane squeezed her hand, her eyes warm and compassionate, but before she could speak, Maria Elena came hurtling through the door, tripped over the trailing laces of her sneakers and landed spreadeagled on the smooth flagstones of the porch. She was up in an instant to throw herself at her mother and hug her around the waist. "Bertha says does she mash the avocados?" she said breathlessly.

Gently Jane disengaged herself, shook her head at the new scrape showing red and raw just below the plaster on Maria Elena's right knee, and stood, laughter giving her face a beauty that, like her young daughter's was not ordinarily apparent. "If at all possible, Glorie, hock the silver and buy stock in a first aid company. We buy plaster strips by the case and antiseptic by the gallon. Excuse me while I check on lunch and play doctor with this young one."

Gloria smiled as she watched the two go into the house. Then she sat back once more in her chair and listened to the soothing splash of the fountain, trying not to think about what being special to Hank Mason would be like; what it would be like having his kisses in times of joy or stress, having his strong arms holding her in the night.

When Jane returned a few minutes later she walked to the tall wrought-iron gate set into the wall of the courtyard. It looked toward the outbuildings and corrals that were some distance from the house. Gloria, who had followed Jane to the gate, saw Hank and Joaquin bending over the inner works of the truck cab she had noticed on their arrival. The children were nowhere in sight.

Jane put two fingers to her lips and whistled, a shrill piercing blast that made Gloria's ears ring. Immediately, Audie and Jamey came running from around one of the barns and the child, Dreamer, swung down from the low branch of a cottonwood tree.

"Wash your hands for lunch," Jane called to

them. "Darn. The men have the motor running and can't hear me. I'll have to go get them."

"I'll go," Gloria quickly volunteered.

"We'll both go." Jane smiled at her mischievously. "Joaquin bought a new European-made truck for the company and I haven't had a chance to look at it yet. I wonder what Hank thinks of it?"

"I didn't know Hank works on trucks, too," Gloria commented.

Jane looked at her in some surprise. "Joaquin is Hank's partner in the trucking company. Didn't you know?"

Gloria shook her head. Hank was partners in a trucking company? She thought he was a footloose mechanic!

"The main office is in Albuquerque, but Joaquin's favorite part of the business is tinkering on the motors of the tractors. That's what you and I call the truck part of the rig. There's always one or two on the ranch that he's working on. But this one is new and shouldn't need any work. These two little boys just want to play with their new toy."

Her voice had been getting louder and louder so that she could be heard over the roar of the truck as they approached, and when Hank abruptly switched off the motor the words *new toy* rang out in the sudden stillness.

They all laughed and Jane gave her husband an affectionate kiss on the cheek as she wrapped an arm about his waist. "Well, it's true," she defended herself, then ran a critical eye over the cab. "The new logo looks nice anyway."

Gloria, following the direction of her gaze, saw the familiar F and M trucking logo, now streamlined and updated, on the door of the cab. For the first time she realized that it was one of the distinctive black and silver trucks that seemed to dominate the highways.

F and M Trucking was one of the largest such companies in the country! Flannigan and Mason. Of course!

She wondered suddenly how Hank and Joaquin had come to be friends as well as business partners.

The two men seemed to have nothing in common but their love of motors. Joaquin was obviously a devoted family man with a friendly, charismatic personality, while Hank was a loner with a personality that warned most people off. His innate gentleness was a hidden thing, a treasure to be found by those brave enough to search for it.

Jane and Joaquin had found it, and Jamey.

Gloria gazed unseeingly at a cottonwood tree standing in solitary loneliness on the far horizon.

She had never been brave, just stubborn. Not the same thing at all.

Hank watched the expressions flitting over Glorie's features until they settled into wistfulness, making him want to take her into his arms and love her until whatever troubled her sank into oblivion.

Love her physically, that is. He was too smart to be caught in love's emotional trap again.

He might concede that particular feeling wasn't a trap for all men, but with his own background he knew just how easy it was to con him with the lure of home and family.

Once burned and all the rest of that particular cliché. Love was like alcohol. It provided temporary warmth and well-being, but could also cost a man his soul. Like a recovering alcoholic, he knew better than to touch the stuff.

Glorie Pellman could be very, very addictive if he weren't very, very careful.

But surely it couldn't hurt to feel a little *affection* for the woman. That oughtn't get him into any trouble. Glorie was so…gallant, he supposed the word was.

Could Joaquin be right?

Joaquin, for all his movie star looks, had an intuitive mind second to none. It's what made him a successful businessman and rancher. They'd been talking business, then moved on to personal topics when Joaquin brought up the subject of Glorie. Hank had known he would. Was that why he'd come?

"Your Glorie is quite a woman," Joaquin commented, an observation having nothing to do with the motor they both leaned over.

"She's not mine," Hank replied flatly, only to remember how often in his thoughts she was "his" Glorie.

Joaquin reached in and tested the tightness of a bolt with his fingers. "You might be right. She's an independent female, isn't she?"

"Too damn independent. Won't take anybody's help even when she needs it."

Hank handed Joaquin a socket wrench to tighten the bolt that was just a hair too loose.

"Have to admire a woman like that," the other man said reflectively, testing the offending part with his fingers again after his infinitesimal adjustment. "You certainly know what it's like to live with the other kind."

"Glorie's about as far from Marina as two women can get." Now Hank reached in to finger the bolt for tightness. "But she doesn't seem to realize it's okay to take a little help now and then without doing a favor back."

"Oh? That bad, huh?" Joaquin quirked a sardonic eyebrow in Hank's direction, but Hank had lifted his head to stare at the far horizon.

"I bought her groceries because anybody could see when she first got to Tulaca that money was a problem."

"Generous of you."

"Generous, hell! She needed them. But do you know what she went and did?"

Fascinated, Joaquin shook his head.

"The damn fool woman *paid* me for them!"

"Took guts," Joaquin murmured.

"Then I fixed her plumbing," Hank added, his tone aggrieved.

"And?"

"She nursed me through the flu. I've never been so embarrassed."

"No kidding?"

"So help me. I took her boy fishing..."

Joaquin gazed at Hank in astonishment, his surprise genuine this time.

"And she fixes supper. This after cooking all the damn day at Mom's Café. I'm telling you, Flannigan, she won't take a thing without giving something back. Usually twice as much."

Sounds like somebody else I know. Hank saw the thought and the wry affection written all over Joaquin's face.

Aloud his friend said, "I think she just likes you.

The things you're talking about are just what one person does for another, no strings.''

"Nice women don't like me," Hank replied. "Except Jane, but she likes everybody."

"She didn't like Marina. And what about your secretary? She worships the ground you walk on." Joaquin had his head under the hood again, his face hidden from view.

"I pay Ms. Jenkens a small fortune to worship the ground I walk on," Hank replied dryly. "And you can get your head out from inside that motor. Most nice women don't like me because I don't like them."

Joaquin grinned at him. "But you like Glorie Pellman." Then dared, "Maybe more than like."

"I like Glorie Pellman," Hank conceded. "And I like her son, Jim. Now drop it, Flannigan."

But Joaquin couldn't let it go just yet. "I think she likes you, too, Mason. Maybe more than likes. Now what are you going to do about it?"

"I think you're crazy," Hank had replied, and changed the subject. He'd heard what he wanted to hear. And he didn't know what the hell he was going to do about it.

But moments before the women joined them, Joaquin had said over the roar of the truck's motor, "Who gives what to whom when doesn't matter a damn, Hank, when the feeling is there. The right partner doesn't keep score."

Chapter Nine

"Four against four, boys against girls," Audie announced, leading the way to the improvised baseball diamond at the side of the house, his bat slung over his shoulder with a couple of worn fielders' gloves hung on it. The children had begged for a game now that they had enough people to "really play."

"Uncle Hank pitches. I play first base. Jim plays third, and Dad plays outfield and second base," he decreed, sizing up his team with an appraising eye.

"Your uncle Hank better not play, Audie," Gloria broke into his plans. "He injured his hand yesterday." She had noticed Hank favoring his hand for the past few hours and the side of his palm was still badly swollen.

"Okay," Audie conceded immediately. "Dad pitches, plays outfield and covers second base. He's our best player," he explained to Jamey who looked both thrilled and apprehensive at playing a team sport for the first time.

"I'll pitch, Audie," Hank said decisively, and turned to give Gloria a hard look. "Pitching a softball to a bunch of women isn't going to cripple me for life, sweetheart."

Gloria glared back at him, hands on her hips, eyes shooting golden fire. "I'm a darn good batter, I'll have you know, *darling*. And if you take another knock on that hand you might very well be crippled for life."

Joaquin's coughing fit filtered into the sudden silence and Gloria's eyes left Hank's to see Jane having difficulty keeping a straight face.

"Sweetheart? Darling?" Jane asked the two of them with assumed puzzlement and madly dancing eyes.

Oh, Lord. She'd completely forgotten the presence of the others. Gloria swallowed. Hank would never forgive her that "darling" remark.

Heat washed her face, having nothing to do with the late afternoon sun.

A similar hint of color lay under Hank's tanned features, though his face wore its usual lack of expression.

"He calls me chauvinist names when he thinks I'm meddling in his business," she told Jane with a touch of defiance, and the truth of the words hit her even as they left her mouth. Every time Hank talked to her in a way he knew she disliked, he was, in effect, putting up verbal barriers.

She looked at him and smiled slowly. It was a barrier that would never fool her again, nor would any of the other meaningless verbiage he threw at her. How could she have been so dense?

Come to think of it, it had been a long time since she'd really paid attention to his hollow wall of words, anyway.

Suddenly full of a cocky happiness, she added aloud for good measure, "And if he can dish it out, he should darn sure be able to take it."

"Sounds reasonable to me," Jane agreed, grinning openly at Hank who now glared at Joaquin as the other man studiedly pulled on a glove, his handsome face the picture of innocence, his lips twitching.

"Gloria's right," she continued matter-of-factly. "You have no business playing infield with your hand still swollen. We need a catcher for both teams and an umpire. You're it."

Giving him no time for argument, she added in a loud stage whisper to the members of her team, "Watch out for him, girls. He cheats."

Hank had the grace to know when he was beaten and watched with an umpire's hawk eye as Audie and Jane stacked hands up the bat handle to see who would bat first: Jane's hand capped the end.

Before he went to take his place on the pitcher's mound, Joaquin spoke low-voiced to Hank but loud enough for his wife to hear, "She cheats, too, darling," and winked.

Gloria's cockiness slid down to the insides of her tennies. Perhaps she'd rubbed it in a bit much. Would a long-standing friendship end today because of her big mouth?

"I didn't mean to cause you embarrassment," she apologized softly as Jane gave a couple of practice swings with the bat.

To her surprise, a quick grin split Hank's austere face. "I never deliver what I can't take, Glorie."

Not since her own childhood did Gloria have as much fun as she did that afternoon. Hank cheated outrageously, giving the children unlimited "Strike Twos" and getting in the path of the adults as they ran toward home plate so the small players had time to get them out. Both teams shouted at and argued with their opponents and tried to top each other's insults. Sometimes Gloria could hardly swing her bat for laughing at the comments flying at her from the other team, Jamey's as loud as the rest.

"She's no batter, she's no batter," he chanted, quickly picking up the jargon of the field. "Easy out, easy out."

At one point she ran toward home plate, turning her head as she ran to follow the progress of her hit in the field, and ran full-tilt into Hank, sending them both crashing to the earth in a tangle of arms and legs.

Sprawled across Hank's chest, she convulsed with laughter, trying to get her breath at the same time.

Hank grinned up into her dusty, sweat-streaked face. "Flirting with the umpire will get you nowhere, Glorie. You're still out."

"I was safe by a mile and you know it!" she argued heatedly, scrambling to her feet. She put out a hand to hoist him up.

Once on his feet, Hank looked down at her as he tossed the ball up and down with his good hand and silently shook his head, grinning.

Gloria, however, wasn't the least intimidated. She shook a fist. "Hank Mason, you're cheating *again!*"

He sighed lustily. "Ah, what the heck," and kissed her quickly on the mouth. "Safe, then."

She had no time to savor the kiss, though her mouth tingled with the small, laughing caress.

"No mushy stuff," Audie yelled from the field.

"Interference with the umpire!" called Joaquin.

"Ah, Mom. Good grief!" from Jamey.

"It's my time to bat," complained Maria Elena softly, standing beside home plate and tugging at Gloria's shorts.

"If I kiss you, can I be safe, too, Uncle Hank?" asked Dreamer.

"Sure," Hank replied amiably. "I'm always available for bribery from pretty girls." He bent so that Dreamer could buss him on the cheek. Maria Elena followed suit and added a fierce hug. Laughing, Jane kissed him, also.

Joaquin made noises of mock anger from the field and Gloria laughed with the rest, but it was an effort. The sight of Jane's small animated face so close to Hank's wiped away her pleasure in the moment.

The game ended not long after when one of the Flannigans' golden labradors stole the ball and led the children of both teams on a merry chase over the desert to recover it. In the meantime the adults flopped down in the shade of one of the tall cottonwoods to cool off with frosty cans of beer.

Joaquin passed the cold, sweating can over his forehead and grinned at his wife sprawled on her tummy beside him. "You're getting old, Janet, missing that easy pop fly."

"I had the sun in my eyes," Jane replied smoothly. "What's your excuse for striking out, old man?" Then wickedly answered her own question, her voice chorusing with Joaquin's, "My trick knee."

They all laughed.

"Joaquin injured his knee in a truck accident several years ago and it's been his excuse ever since," Jane explained to Gloria.

"And Janet never lets an old cowboy like me get away with it," Joaquin added mournfully.

Gloria, sitting with her back against the rough bark of the tree, started to chuckle but it was cut off abruptly as Hank, who had been sitting beside her, suddenly swiveled around and put his head in her lap.

She caught her breath at the warm intimate pressure of his head against her abdomen, but when she looked down into his face it told her nothing, for his thick curling incongruous lashes were lowered and his mouth blandly relaxed.

Lifting blank unseeing eyes to the far empty horizon, Gloria fought the urge to bend down and touch his lips with her own and let the teasing kiss of earlier deepen into something much, much more.

In an effort to pull herself together she looked at Jane and asked the first thing that popped into her head. "Joaquin calls you Janet. Is that your given name?"

The other woman laughed softly and her hand went out just as her husband's hand came forward to take it. "No. My given name is Jane. A fortune teller confused Joaquin in his early years."

"I've told you, darlin', it was your mother who was confused. You were misnamed." The tone was teasing and obviously this was an obscure family joke, but Joaquin and Jane exchanged a look of such loving intensity that Gloria's eyes dropped, as if she were an inadvertent witness to a passionate embrace.

She found herself looking into Hank's black gaze and saw herself reflected there, a vulnerable, frightened woman who confronted life with a small son, a pugnacious chin, and a lonely heart. She frowned. Had this man somehow created the disgusting image?

Hank, however, merely gazed back at her and smiled his slow devastating smile, so that Gloria's mouth, acting with a will of its own, smiled back at him…and she watched in wonder as the woman reflected in his eyes suddenly looked confident and happy.

And loved.

Gloria through the looking glass, she thought whimsically of the illusion that could only be a trick of the light, and took a sip of her beer.

The children, with the softball recovered, came running to join them and Bertha brought out a frosty pitcher of lemonade as the adults had another beer.

The afternoon stretched pleasantly into an equally relaxed evening with a long informal family dinner, an hour of television, baths, and finally bed for the children.

Jane and Gloria came back into the living room after making sure the children were settled for the night, Jane plopping down on the sofa beside her husband, Gloria taking an armchair that paired with Hank's.

"They're such angels when they're asleep." Jane grinned at Gloria and Gloria smiled back, both of them knowing the boys, at least, would be awake for some time, judging by the muffled giggling coming from Audie's room.

Bertha brought in coffee and the talk ranged over many topics, the Flannigans both widely read. Hank, Gloria noticed, had no trouble holding his own in conversation that meandered through politics, entertainment, and social issues.

At one point Joaquin remarked, "Ted Bissell will be here in the morning to pick up the Mustang. Are you going to take the T-Bird back to Tulaca, or do you want to use my Buick?"

"I'll take the Buick if it won't be an inconvenience," Hank answered. "With only two seats, the T-Bird doesn't have much room for two adults, a kid, and a pup." One of the labrador puppies had found its way into Jamey's heart and eventually into his possession.

"No, it won't make any difference to us. Around here, there's always something to drive. Jane will love an excuse to use the pickup."

Gloria was puzzled. "Is something wrong with the Mustang?"

"Since I sold it, I hope not," Hank answered laconically.

"But why did you sell it? It drives like a dream and now you have the interior looking nice. It doesn't even smell anymore." She wondered what she'd said to make the others laugh.

"I hope Ted Bissell will be as enthusiastic. He's the buyer and I'm taking a large chunk of his cash."

Finally he took pity on her complete loss. "I restore classic automobiles and sell them as a hobby," he explained. "Joaquin found the Thunderbird for me about a month ago, parked and rusting in a back lot in Arizona, complete with stray cat and a litter of kittens. It's a two seater, a 1957 model. The kind actresses drove in the heyday of the Hollywood starlet and their beefcake boyfriends.''

He grinned. ''So it smells a little of cat and doesn't look like much, but when I finish with it, it will look exactly the same or better than it did when it came from the factory. If possible, I use all original parts, from the radio knobs to the cap on the radiator. How about a ride tomorrow?''

Gloria pretended to consider. ''I don't know. I warn you, I'm not adopting any kittens.''

''All in loving homes,'' Hank countered easily.

''Well, in that case…''

She excused herself for the night a while later, pleading tiredness. Jane decided to do likewise and the two women once more checked on the children, covering the boys who had fallen asleep amid a fleet of miniature cars piled in the bed with them.

Gloria was tired, but as she lay in her wide, comfortable bed in a pleasant bedroom decorated in the classically simple style of the American Southwest, she found that her mind would not relinquish the many and varied events of the day. She thought of how Jamey had blossomed among the friendly, uninhibited Flannigan children; and of Jane and Joaquin and the love that obviously permeated every aspect of their marriage, though they teased and argued constantly.

A force field of love encircles this house, she thought with a touch of envy. No wonder Hank is a different person here. She had never heard him talk so much, laugh so much. Was it because of his feelings for Jane?

The thought depressed her. She wanted Hank to find someone to love who would love him back. He was a good man, the best of men, worthy of a woman's unselfish love.

More than worthy. Hank had so much strength. Inside that granite face of his, so much gentleness. But most of all, he was brimming with love. And watching him share those qualities openhandedly with friends made Gloria's heart tremble when she thought of what he would share with his chosen woman.

Lucky, lucky woman.

Throwing back the light coverings, she left the bed to stand for a long moment with her forehead pressed against a cool pane of glass in the French door opening onto the porch surrounding the courtyard.

And wasn't she, too, worthy? Didn't she deserve to be loved with warmth and gentleness...and a fiery passion needing no expression in bruising violence?

She shook her head at her thoughts and smiled in derisive self-mockery. What had happened to the woman who swore never to have another thing to do with men; for whom it would be a cold day on the Sahara before she would marry again?

Picking up the light wrap matching her gown, Gloria shrugged into it, then opened the French doors and stepped into the chilly desert darkness. The muted splash of the fountain seemed an echo to the cold twinkling stars spangling the night.

Where was the bitter, cynical woman she'd been before meeting—she stopped the budding thought, completing it on another track—before she'd moved to Tulaca?

Having a mountain for a friend and neighbor

seemed to have a softening effect on her, she thought, then chuckled soundlessly. She was thinking like Hank, giving the mountain character and personality.

Inhaling clear air tasting like cold spring water, she savored the dusky odor of roses climbing over a nearby trellis.

A frisson of awareness trickled down her neck. Turning slowly, she saw Hank, as if summoned by her thoughts, standing near the shadow of the rose trellis. The imaginative child she'd once been wondered if he were real. She faced him over the few feet separating them, not speaking, thought and breathing suspended.

Slowly he reached up and broke off a rose with a small snap. Then without sound, a being of the night, he walked toward her until he stood so close she could smell the clean fresh scent of him touched with an undercurrent of whiskey and the rose in his hand.

Still without speaking, he placed the rose over her ear in the massed darkness of her hair and with the side of his finger, lifted her chin to study her face.

Only then did her whole mind believe in his reality.

"Now you look like a Mexican *señorita,*" he said softly. "Waiting for your lover. Dark and wild and lovely, but virginal in your long white gown and with your hair hanging down your back."

Mesmerized by his soft seductive drawl, Gloria could only focus on the lazy sensual lips so close to her own, watching their movement as he formed his words.

"The flower goes behind the other ear for a woman no longer a girl," she said. "Virgins don't have five-year-old children.'' She tried to speak with her usual flippancy, but the words came out a husky whisper.

It was completely beyond her to avert her eyes from his.

Hank tucked the flower more firmly behind her ear and ran his hand over the hair framing her face. ''The rose is where it belongs, Glorie,'' he said softly. ''You've been grossly handled but never touched, I think.''

Bending, he laid his lips on hers gently, sampling their sweetness, before pulling back and studying the soft vulnerability of her face once more. Her lips were slightly parted and inviting, her lashes half closed over slumberous eyes, the face of a girl poised and waiting.

The man studying it felt a clutch in his midsection.

Slowly he lowered his face to hers a second time, his mouth tentative, questioning. The lips under his formed a sweet responsive pressure of their own.

Hank lightly encircled her slim shoulders, allowing her to slip away if that was her wish, but instead he felt the white-hot touch of her breasts against his chest as her hands splayed over his lower back.

Suddenly, in silent, glorious, soul-deep exultation, something trapped deep inside, raging and struggling for weeks, for a lifetime, broke free and Hank's hold tightened convulsively as the kiss deepened.

Without hesitation, Gloria flew with him, flew high and effortlessly.

His mouth never leaving hers, he swept her into his arms and carried her through the open doors to her bedroom.

A cool breath of sanity touched him. Still holding

her in his arms, he lifted his mouth from hers and asked softly but flatly, "Is this what you want, Glorie?"

Her forehead rested against the side of his neck in the place made for it. When she spoke, her warm breath bathed his skin. "Yes, Hank. This is what I want," she said, her voice husky but as flat as his own.

He released the breath he hadn't realized he held and slowly lowered her feet to the floor, before untying the ribbons holding the wrap together at her throat and just over her breasts. Her gown had a shallow scooped neckline and was of a soft cotton batiste so that her breasts showed shadowy pink and firm against their thin covering. When he closed his mouth over their tips, the material became damply transparent, the blatant thrusts of the nipples against the wet fabric becoming a flirtation pulsing hotly through his loins.

Her hands came up to pull his shirt from his jeans and then to slowly unbutton it, sliding it with warm caresses from his shoulders and slipping it carefully over his injured hand. His breath stopped as her tongue sampled a nipple and warm fingers slipped just under the back waistband of his low-riding jeans, feathering over the swell of his buttocks.

With fumbling fingers he unbuckled his belt and unsnapped his pants, lowering them until he wore nothing but his silk continental briefs.

All the while she watched him, her face soft and warm and bemused, as if his body were a precious gift to her.

No woman had ever looked at him like that! Women had looked at his body with lust and with pleasure, but none had ever looked on it as if he needn't do anything at all but be who he was.

When she reached out and touched him, the world stopped.

Once more his tongue teased a hard nipple through the soft stuff of her gown before he slowly pulled the thin material over her head as if lifting a drape to reveal a work of art. Glorie's slim perfection had decorated his days for weeks, haunted his nights, and made other, easier women slip into inadequacy. Now he saw what before he'd only imagined, her body's perfect symmetry, the small high-pointed breasts balanced by a slim waist, flat stomach, and taut rounded buttocks.

He ran the flat of his hand gently over the swell of her breasts, down over her smooth stomach and caught his fingers in the band of her bikini panties, pulling them down until she stood before him proud and naked, her head thrown back to accept the warm darkness of his gaze.

No coy flutterings from his Glorie, his glory. No false modesty or shyly lowered lashes. He took her mouth with fierce possessiveness, one hand threaded through the thick wild lushness of her hair, the other arm around her shoulders. Her mouth came up to meet his and once more he felt her arms about his waist, holding him with unexpected strength, as if she would bind him to her and never let him go.

After this night, would he ever be free?

Did he want to be?

Through the open French doors the fountain splashed its harmony with the stars and the faint smell of climbing roses filled the night. Or perhaps it was the scent of the flower now lying forgotten on the bedroom floor.

Gloria reveled in Hank's hands stroking her so surely. Her body leapt and danced to the music as his supple fingers played over it, into it, bringing her to joy, to madness, to womanly fulfillment.

In counterpoint, her lips limned Hank's face, his wonderful face, like no other face on earth in its beauty. Her fingers traced his body, wandering, wondering, rejoicing in its strength, in its compatibility with her softness.

Man and woman joined, became the Universal One, where no part dominated, no part subjected. Where one part led, the other guided. One part formed melody, the other rhythm. They danced the movements prescribed by nature, but themselves created the music to which they danced, knowing it to be like no other in their experience or ever in the world.

Gloria lay, languorous and sated, in the curve of Hank's arm. She had dozed lightly but awakened, aware that Hank was not asleep. "What is it?" she whispered.

He kissed her forehead. "Nothing. Go back to sleep."

She raised her head to look into his face, illuminated in the faint moonlight. "You should take one of the pills the doctor gave you."

He smiled, and automatically her fingers arrived to trace the curve of his mouth as if to capture the devastation of it. He kissed her fingers.

"I'll take one later, Glorie. I drank a couple of whiskeys with Joaquin just before I came out on the porch. If I mix the two I'm likely to reenact La Dolce Vita in the fountain. The pills are in the pocket of my jeans. When the whiskey is no longer a factor, I'll take one. I'm fine.''

With the good fingers on his injured hand he reached up and smoothed the tumbled hair back from her face. ''With you beside me, who needs pills anyway?'' He tugged her hair gently until her head lowered and her mouth covered his. Her hair spilled around them in a curtain, giving the immediate flare of passion a feeling of hidden intimacy.

Later, Gloria awoke again, lying in the curve of Hank's body, spoon fashion. Though she couldn't see him, she knew at once he was still awake.

Without a word, she pulled away from the arms encircling her and left the bed, padding around it till she came to the heap of their clothing. She felt around in the darkness, picked up Hank's jeans and fished in the pocket for the plastic container of pills, then went into the adjoining bathroom, switched on the light, and came out with a glass of water. Going to the bed, she stood beside it until Hank sat up.

''Damn, you're bossy,'' he muttered grumpily as she shook one of the white tablets into his outstretched palm.

She didn't answer, but took the glass back into the bathroom when he had finished with it, switched off the light, and climbed back into bed.

Hank received her into his arms as she assumed her former position. ''Your feet are cold,'' he murmured into her ear. ''In fact, you're deliciously cold all over.'' His warm fingers toyed with the nub of her nipple that the cold had raised.

She rubbed a cold foot over the inside of his leg and he yelped.

"I'll get you for that," he growled, biting her shoulder gently, but he tucked his warm feet under her cold ones.

He held her close, allowing the warmth of his body to absorb the chill of hers, and cradled her long after her small shivers had dissipated, enjoying the silken length of her body against his own and the scent of her recently shampooed hair in his nostrils until the throb in his hand became a dull ache, and then merely uncomfortable, and he finally slept.

With his soft intermittent rumblings in her ear, Gloria, too, slipped into slumber at last, warm, infinitely comfortable, and at peace.

She awakened when Hank left the bed, the room still in darkness. Was he going back to his own bedroom? A chill seemed to flow under the covers where his warm body had been.

"Get up, Glorie. Let's go."

"Where?" she asked in surprise and sat up.

He chuckled and pulled on his jeans. "We're going for a ride in the Thunderbird."

"But...but it's night!"

"No, it isn't. It's almost dawn. Get a move on, but bring a jacket. The T-Bird doesn't have a top."

"I didn't bring a jacket," she told him as she scrambled into a pair of jeans herself. He flipped on the bathroom light and it spilled its radiance into the bedroom.

Suddenly Gloria felt uncomfortable dressing with Hank in the room, especially as she could feel his dark eyes touching her as he buttoned his shirt.

It was ridiculous to feel so uptight, she told herself.

By now the man knew every inch of her body intimately, as she knew his. But the night was over and gone with it was the feeling that Hank Mason was the other half of her.

"You can use mine. I'll be warm enough." He went to get his jacket for her and she felt a faint relief at his going. Quickly she ran a brush through her hair and braided it into one thick plait, then hurriedly splashed her face and brushed her teeth. When she emerged from the bathroom she found Hank waiting for her in the still darkened bedroom.

He switched off the bathroom light and before her eyes could adjust to the darkness, bundled her without ceremony into his jacket. Taking her hand he pulled her toward the patio door.

Gloria dug in her heels. "Hank, I can't *see*," she hissed, a confused part of her rebelling at being maneuvered willy-nilly.

"Sure you can." She heard the light laughter in his voice just before his mouth homed in to touch hers gently…and abruptly, for he had her by the hand again, pulling her out the door and through the dark courtyard, the fountain splashing in merry delight.

For a moment the magic of the night glittered between them, long enough for Gloria to allow herself to be pulled along, her steps running to keep up with Hank's long strides, through the outer gate and over the path to the stable that had been converted into a large garage.

While she waited by the garage door, Hank went in and backed out a long, low, heavy-looking sports car bearing a vague resemblance to a squared-off rocket and told her to climb in—literally, because the door on the passenger side had no handle of any sort.

"What will Jane and Joaquin think when they find us gone?" Gloria asked breathlessly, swinging her legs over the windowsill in one smooth motion and settling herself into a bucket seat that smelled of dust and decay and mildew...and cat. In the darkness it was difficult to see the interior of the car but she had the impression of age and misuse.

"They know you're with me," Hank answered matter-of-factly, backing the car expertly around in a semicircle and heading out of the drive with speed. "This is a working ranch, remember? Joaquin was in the kitchen when I went to get a flask of coffee from Bertha."

"But I can't just go off and leave Jamey."

"Relax, Glorie. We'll be back in an hour. Jim won't even be up by then."

"Nevertheless, I'd rather go back," Gloria answered, feeling guilty because she knew, even as the words left her mouth, that she lied.

The cold air whipped against her face and hair but she didn't feel it. She felt instead a huge hole of bleakness where her heart should be; felt as if she'd been betrayed in some way into acting out of character; felt as if control of her actions and emotions had once more slipped from her fingers.

She also felt Hank's instant withdrawal. One second a warm vibrant friend sat beside her; the next, the cold impersonal stranger she had met so long ago on the mountain.

He drove in silence a few more minutes, then began to slow.

She knew she shouldn't blame Hank for her ambivalent feelings. At no time had he forced her, had even shown commendable restraint in the early stages of their lovemaking. She was the one who had tossed reason aside, willingly forgetting under the insidious magic of his touch, that Hank Mason needed, really needed, no one.

But Hank wasn't slowing the car to turn around. He was stopping.

Glancing around, she became aware of being in the middle of nowhere, all about them nothing but shadowy emptiness. Silence descended when he cut the motor.

Gloria licked dry lips. "Hank…"

"Be quiet," he ordered softly, but with such controlled hostility that her teeth snapped together.

He sat looking straight ahead and after a moment of studying his shadowed form, she turned her face to the front, also.

Hank had parked the car facing east. As the sky lightened and snuffed out the stars, she became aware of a low range of mountains in front of them, their peaks thrown first into silhouette by the rising sun and then illuminated, changing colors a dozen times as the sun climbed the horizon. The desert and its sparse vegetation became an ever-changing canvas as clear, warming light performed the artistry it had been practicing for eons.

Unconsciously, Gloria leaned forward, lips slightly parted in wonder at the spectacular display of the dawn. Only when the sun was well over the mountains did she sit back with a little sigh.

"No wonder Georgia O'Keeffe painted the desert," she said softly, turning to Hank with shining eyes. With surprise she saw that her hand gripped the top of his injured one where it loosely held the lower curve of the steering wheel.

"No wonder," Hank agreed softly, his lashes lowered as he, too, looked at the small capable hand covering his. Then his black gaze swept up to meet hers and she felt a jolt right down to her toes as he smiled. "Everyone should see the sun rise over the desert at least once in their lives."

He seemed to sigh quietly, or perhaps it was a whisper of the desert. "Shall we go back? You were only abducted for a sunrise."

His hand left the steering wheel and hers fell away as he reached for the ignition key.

"Yes… No!" She caught the forward thrust of his arm before he could start the motor. "I mean…" She floundered in the face of his lifted brows. "Thank you for bringing me, Hank. It was beautiful and unforgettable. A while ago, I…I just didn't feel right about leaving Jamey."

He turned to her then, his face momentarily suffused with an anger quickly erased before he said tiredly, "Come off it, Gloria. Like a *nice* woman, you're just not feeling right about last night."

He turned the ignition key and the motor came to rattling, noisy life. Stepping on the clutch, he put the car in gear with an uncharacteristic jerk, made a tight U-turn, and headed back down the road they'd come.

From surprise, Gloria went straight on to glorious, furious anger. She leaned over, turned the key, and removed it from the ignition.

If she expected an immediate response from Hank, it wasn't forthcoming. He merely shifted into neutral without comment and allowed the car to glide to a smooth stop.

"I ought to warn you," he then said mildly, "that if you're planning on adding dramatic interest to this charade by throwing the key out the window, you'll have a ten-mile walk back to the ranch. That key is the only one there is.''

"Don't be silly," Gloria snapped. "I just want your undivided attention." She slapped the key angrily onto the dashboard within his reach. In one lithe movement she hoisted herself onto the door frame and swung her legs over.

Hank, not knowing what to expect, pushed himself up to sit on the back of the convertible, watching her warily as she stalked around the front of the car and came to glare up at him.

"How dare you presume to judge me!" she spat. "Suppose I do feel a little strange. My God, I don't go bed-hopping every night and I have a young son to consider. But I'm not sorry about what happened. Don't you dare try to make it into something sordid and...and ugly. It wasn't!"

Suddenly the flashing gold in her eyes seemed to dim as she searched his face for a long, silent moment.

"Was it?" she asked at last, uncertainty coloring the low-voiced question.

Hank, staring down into her searching face, let out a small sigh and ran his hand through his hair. "No, it wasn't sordid. And it sure as hell wasn't ugly," he said gruffly. He, too, swung his legs over and pushed himself off the car.

By unspoken consent they began walking side by side along the faint track leading off into the desert, the soft rhythmic crunch of their footsteps the only sound.

"Since we've agreed last night wasn't so bad,"

Hank said at last, "do you want to tell me what's wrong?"

They stopped, two figures in a vast sunlit expanse fast losing the crisp chill of early dawn. Hank's face held no expression, but there was an unnerving stillness about him.

"Last night we were two lonely people in a house full of love," she tried to explain, though none of her words defined what she really wanted to say at all. "For a while we needed each other in the most elemental way possible. But it's daylight now and…"

"And you don't need me anymore," Hank finished dryly, without heat or anger. Was there a hint of relief?

Gloria turned away from him to face the far-distant desert mountains shimmering now against a cerulean sky, letting the words go unchallenged.

"We're two of a kind," she said at last. "Prickly, untrusting, independent. That's what seems to work best for people like ourselves. I didn't want you suddenly thinking we have to be a…a couple."

He looked at her long and hard and she withstood his scrutiny stoically, hoping nothing of her jumbled feelings showed in her face. When he turned away and they began walking back toward the car, she felt confident her secret was safe.

The morning had warmed rapidly and she shrugged out of Hank's denim jacket as they walked. He took it from her and hooked it over his shoulder with the good fingers of his injured hand.

God, you're an accomplished liar and a master hypocrite, Gloria told herself acidly as she climbed into the convertible. She closed her eyes briefly. But worst of all, you're a fool.

The slamming of Hank's door seemed to punctuate the thought.

She loved him.

Why hadn't she known or guessed? How had love crept in so quietly, hiding away in her heart until a desert sunrise illumined it in all its stark, frightening beauty? She loved Hank Mason with a deep burning passion already consuming her.

How could she have been so unaware of its painful existence? Since her fall on the mountain when Hank's arms had cradled her as he carried her to his cabin, she could not remember a time when she had not loved him. Yet she hadn't known.

Blissfully unaware, she'd erected wall after wall between them, only to have one of his kisses tumble those fragile barriers to the dust they were made of. Who was she kidding? One of his rare *smiles* was as potent to her heart as meaningless diamonds had ever been from Eric. And she hadn't known.

She glanced at Hank's hard, delineated profile. He sat easily behind the wheel, the big old-fashioned car responding under his sure control as nimbly as its age and abuse would permit. Though he looked cynically aloof, Gloria sensed a fine tension in him that matched her own.

Pretending to gaze out the window at the deceptively empty land flashing by, she saw instead, in her mind's eye, his craggy dark features that could lighten to such soft sensuality when he smiled.

Why had her unwary heart chosen Hank, she thought sadly, who gave his smiles with the same frugality other men gave thousand dollar bills, and his love not at all?

Chapter Ten

Later that morning Gloria drifted into the kitchen for another cup of coffee. The room was empty, Bertha off in another part of the house and Jane was with Maria Elena and Dreamer, consoling the girls after Mari had found a dead baby bird on the veranda.

Pouring her coffee from a pot kept going throughout the day, she cradled the mug in her palms and surveyed the spotless kitchen. Light streamed through its windows, set in two-foot-thick adobe walls, and Indian and Mexican pots lined the mantel of the rounded Southwestern style fireplace in one corner. Bright red chili *ristras* hung from exposed roof beams and an old-fashioned blue crockery bowl piled high with fruit sat in the center of the massive kitchen table.

This was a beautiful home, she thought. What she

wouldn't give for one like it. No, not a two hundred-year-old Spanish hacienda. Any style of house would be home to her if it held the same love and laughter as this one. Even an isolated one-room cabin on a mountain would be home then.

She wandered to the sink, still cradling her coffee, and peered out the window there. Jamey and Audie were playing an improvised game near the front curving driveway where the Mustang was parked awaiting the arrival of the Bissells. Their game involved a large red ball, lots of running, and lots of shouting. She watched them play without really seeing them. Tears turned her heart to a soggy thumping thing, but her eyes remained dry.

In her imagination, she saw two small boys join the game with Audie and Jamey, boys with shocks of straight black hair and night-black eyes, all knobby knees and sharp elbows. Boys who would grow up laughing, secure in the knowledge of their parents' love for them and for each other. And she, the boys' wise, all-knowing mother, would also know herself loved by her boisterous boys, and cherished by her long, lean, black-eyed husband.

Gloria fought the urge to giggle at her silly imaginings, and discovered her soggy heart was fast wringing itself out into her eyes.

Hank, the lover? Oh, yes. Definitely yes.

Hank, the husband? Hardly.

Hank, the father? Never.

"Glorie?"

Tepid coffee sloshed over her hand and into the sink as she jumped, startled. Furiously blinking the thin film of moisture from her eyes, she poured the rest of the coffee down the drain and rinsed her hand, snapping off a paper towel from a convenient roll before slowly turning to confront the man of her thoughts, standing now just behind her.

"Sorry," Hank said ruefully. "I didn't mean to..." He caught sight of her face. "What's wrong?"

Her chin lifted, a gesture he knew well, and he sighed soundlessly. He knew what was wrong. How could something that seemed so right, that for the first time in years made his life feel complete, how could all that rightness have hurt this woman so badly? A woman, furthermore, for whom he'd rather die himself than cause the smallest hint of discomfort?

How long had it been since he'd felt about a woman the way he did Glorie Pellman? Had he *ever* felt this way?

Affection, he guessed, was stronger than he thought if it got him all bent out of shape because of a woman's misty eyes.

Unknowingly, he frowned. "Don't look like that," he ordered gruffly.

Gloria stiffened at the tone and her chin ratcheted up another notch. She drew welcome anger around her like a cloak of mail and did her best to stare the man down. The boys' shrill voices drifted into the tension-filled kitchen. "You have no right—" she began hotly.

"What in the hell?" Hank stared over her shoulder, his face no longer frowning but filled with all the potential destruction of a thundercloud at what he saw out the window.

"Those kids are food for buzzards," he muttered ominously.

Turning, Gloria, too, looked out to see what had

put Hank in such a sudden tizzy...and was just in time to see Audie race madly to the rear fender of the Mustang, slap it with one dusty paw, and turn to begin the flight to home base.

Jamey clutched the red ball and she could almost see his indecision as to what to do with it, whether he should try to tag Audie before the older boy could get to base or race him to get there first. In a fit of indecisive excitement, he suddenly threw the ball at Audie instead.

It missed the laughing boy by a wide margin, but hit against the door panel of the Mustang with a resounding thud.

And then Hank was there.

Even from the kitchen window, Gloria could see the anger radiating from him. He towered over the two boys and she saw the instant stillness in their faces...and the absolute terror building in Jamey's.

"Oh, my God," she breathed, and tore out of the kitchen.

She hit the outside door just in time to hear Hank's drawl roll over the two youngsters like an enveloping blanket of soft menace. "I am *really* mad," he said, and she knew, and the boys knew, he really was.

Something in Jamey's flickering gaze must have given warning because Hank skewered the two in front of him with a look and ordered, "Don't move," before turning squarely to the woman on the porch.

His face, his fortress face, stopped her cold. Was it hurt she saw behind it?

"I'm not Eric," he said.

The softly spoken words cut through the air like a sword in the hands of a samurai. He turned back to the boys and only then did Gloria realize she held the kitchen broom in her hand. She didn't remember picking it up.

"Look at my car," Hank growled at the boys.

Obediently, they turned to gaze at the Mustang. But first Jamey flicked a glance at Audie, who looked cautious and chastened, perhaps even a little worried, but certainly not afraid. Jamey did his best to copy the six-year-old's expression exactly, but his heart thumped like a trip-hammer and he fought the sudden urge to go to the bathroom.

Then he had the comforting thought that perhaps he was more afraid of wetting his pants than he was of Hank's anger.

"Well?"

"It's a nice car, Uncle Hank," Audie offered tentatively. "What kind is it?"

"It's a Mustang." In his surprise that his new friend and instant hero didn't know such an important fact, Jamey answered before Hank could, with a touch of male pride, "A '65."

Hank folded his arms, his cold gaze bringing the boys back to the point. "What's wrong with my '65 Mustang?"

"Nothing," Audie said. "It's really a great car, Uncle Hank. Great color, too. Bright red."

But Jamey knew what was wrong with it. Hadn't he sat with Hank while he waxed the new paint job to a shiny gloss? "It's dirty," he said softly, surveying the smudges over the backside of the car, the handprints and smears, and the round dusty signature the ball had left each time it hit the bright red finish.

He hung his head.

"And if one of you had let go a power throw, what might have happened?" Hank asked sternly.

Both boys recognized the compliment for their throwing prowess hidden in the accusing question.

Jamey's head snapped up. "We might have put a dent in it." His bronze eyes glowed at the thought.

"We might have broken a window," Audie breathed. "Or maybe even the *windshield*." The word *awesome* hovered in the air unspoken.

"And you might have lost your allowances for the next six months paying for repairs," Hank inserted coldly, putting a damper on their excited speculations.

Both young heads drooped again.

"As it is, you two are going to wash my car and put it back to its original shine."

The heads snapped up as the boys gazed at each other in delight.

"While I supervise."

Grins disappeared in the reality that if Hank was going to supervise, he wasn't playing around.

Gloria took her broom and went back to the kitchen to put it away as Hank, in the tone of a sergeant major, clipped out orders for fetching buckets, rags, and the garden hose. On the whole, she had to acknowledge that Hank had handled the situation quite well.

Jane was standing at the sink where Gloria had stood just a short time earlier and was also looking out the window. "What's going on?" she asked. "Hank looks like the thunder god's messenger." Then she spotted the broom in Gloria's hand and her brows lifted.

"I...um...thought I'd sweep the porch," Gloria said sheepishly. "The boys, ah, got Hank's Mustang dirty."

"Good Lord. Do they have skin left?"

But Jane didn't sound worried, and Gloria felt even more silly for thinking Hank might seriously have harmed one of the children.

She smiled ruefully. "They're in one piece but they have to wash the car."

The women's eyes met, and clung, and they smiled like conspirators. "Do you suppose Hank has any idea what happens when two boys get around a water hose?" Jane asked mischievously.

Gloria giggled. "I think so. He's going to supervise."

Jane shook her head. "Brave man."

Unable to help herself, a while later Gloria was back on the front porch in a lawn chair, screened by a trellis of morning glory vines that allowed her to see, without being seen, the industriously working boys and the man watching them.

Hank's method of dealing with the boys fascinated her. There was stern masculinity in it, yet a subtle acknowledgment of the boys' pride in themselves. In making them wash the car, he told them they were old enough for such a job, but also made them aware of the hard work they had thoughtlessly ruined.

And she had thought him without parenting skills! Hank would make a wonderful father.

When Audie and Jamey had the car cleaned to his satisfaction, Hank left his spot in the shade and gave each of them a chamois rag, keeping one of the pieces of soft leather for himself.

"Now we dry the water off," he told them. "Jim, you take one side of the car. Audie, take the other. I'll do the top and the hood. Take the chamois like so, and drag it over the car like this." He demon-

strated. "The object is to get the streaks off and make
the car *shine*. Think you can?"

Both boys nodded importantly and the three of
them set about making the Mustang *shine,* conversation flowing easily with the boys' high-pitched
voices shimmering through the clear desert air and
Hank's low rumbling breaking in occasionally to an-
chor the children's penchant for excited flight.

Gloria leaned back in the lawn chair, closed her
eyes, and just listened.

She opened them again as an expectant hush settled over the drive and peered through the vines to
see Hank circling the automobile and surveying it
critically. His ostentatious drama made her smile, but
like the boys she wanted to cheer when he solemnly
declared it now back to the way it was, with the dry
admonishment to "Keep it that way."

"Yes, sir," both boys replied gravely.

Hank coiled the water hose, its nozzle turned off,
as the boys gathered cleaning supplies. Near him,
Jamey picked up the half-full bucket, lifted it high,
and emptied it in a grand waterfall. Water, now full
of red desert grit, bounced off the hard earth and onto
Hank's impeccably shined boots.

Jamey stilled, his guilty eyes fixed on the red mud
marring the hand-tooled leather. Slowly he raised his
head, his gaze leaving the wet boots, following the
long length of Hank's jeans to slide over his low-
riding shiny belt buckle, collide off each pearlized
snap on his Western shirt, slither over an unsmiling
mouth, until they finally fixed on unwinking black
eyes partially hidden behind uncompromising cheekbones.

With his face flushed with heat and his white-blond hair spiked with perspiration, his gaze fixed on Hank's face, and he swallowed.

Gloria held her breath...and saw Jamey's chin lift. "I'm sorry, Hank," her son said. Not in fear, or even embarrassment, but in genuine apology.

Hank smiled the slow lethal smile of his that always stole Gloria's breath, and nodded his head. "Accidents happen, boy."

Before Jamey could respond, however, Audie crept up behind the younger boy and thrust a wet rag down the back of his shirt. "Oh, I'm sorry, Jim," he said outrageously. "It slipped."

For a second Jamey looked stunned. Then he wriggled and pulled the soppy rag from beneath his shirttail.

"Here, let me rinse it out for you," Hank said, taking the wet rag while Jamey was still trying to decide what to do with it. Flicking on the hose nozzle, he held the ensuing powerful jet of water three inches from the rag in his hand, angling it so that the stream ricocheted off it and liberally sprayed the two boys standing next to him.

"Soo-oo sorry," he said innocently when both boys yelled...and caught a dripping sponge right in the midsection.

"Now who would do a nasty thing like that?" Hank asked of no one in particular and, as the boy did his best to look righteous while fighting a fit of the giggles, squeezed the sponge over Jamey's blond head.

From then on it was every man and boy for himself, the air full of water and meaningless apologies.

Gloria stood on the steps watching this scene from a Three Stooges' video and laughed till her sides hurt. Suddenly Jane was beside her, flanked by Dreamer and Maria Elena.

"I knew it," Jane said, shaking her head.

"I want to play, too," Mari said, but before the little girl could join the three in the yard, as yet oblivious to their audience, Jane put her hand on the child's shoulder.

"No, it's almost lunchtime and the Bissells will be here any moment. I'd better end this before we have a flood."

She accomplished her goal by the simple task of walking around the side of the house to the hydrant and turning off the water.

Suddenly Hank was holding a lifeless hose and the boys were staring about in stunned surprise.

"Mudroom," Jane said succinctly.

Catching the eye of his two young companions, Hank shrugged infinitesimally and began recoiling the hose as if he hadn't a care in the world and wasn't standing in the bright sunshine with his black hair plastered to his forehead and water dripping off the tip of his nose. The boys silently picked up their buckets and rags. Then, with Hank leading the way, the three of them filed around to the side of the house and out of sight.

But as they passed in front of Jane, with majestic silence, squishing with each step, first Hank, then Audie, then Jamey handed her their wet and dripping rags so that water streamed over her arms, dripped off her elbows, and plopped drop by drop between her sandaled toes.

"Those rascals," she said indignantly. Her gaze caught Mari's, Dreamer's, and Gloria's open grins and just for a moment she grinned back with all of

Audie's mischievousness, thoughtfully weighing the dripping rags in her palms.

Then she sighed. "Nah, better not. The Bissells. Lunch. Female superiority. Bad aim."

Laughing together, she and Gloria wrung out the cloths and walked around the house to peg them on the back line.

Hank was just buttoning on a dry shirt when Jamey appeared at the open door of his bedroom. The boy stood for a moment with his hands in the back pockets of the fresh pair of jeans Gloria had put on him. "Hank?" he finally said hesitantly.

"Yes, son?"

"You know when we were playing with the water after we cleaned the Mustang?"

"Yes, son?"

"We got it wet again."

"We did?"

"Yes, sir. There's water splashes all over its side."

"Hmm. And Ted Bissell's going to be here pretty soon to pick it up. Want to help me dry it off again right quick?"

"Yes, *sir!*"

In moments the two of them were bent over the near side of the car, chamois skins once more in hand.

"Hank?"

"Yes, son?"

"Am I really your son?"

Hank's arm swiped the soft leather slowly across the width of the door before he settled completely on his hunkers to confront the boy now staring at him so earnestly.

"No, Jim, you're not."

"I wish I was," Jamey said softly.

"I wish you were, too, Jim." Hank had a hard time getting the words out and they came to life sounding rough and hard, but the boy didn't seem to find anything wrong with them.

"I hate my dad. He hurt me and he hurt my mama."

Not Mom. "Mama" he'd said, a small child's frightened remembrance. But Gloria had said she wanted Jim to have good thoughts of his dad, every child's right.

"Hate's a big word," Hank said slowly. He dabbed at a water spot near his shoulder. "You look like your dad, I imagine."

"Mom says I do." Jamey shuffled his feet a little.

"He must have been a handsome man."

Wrinkling his nose, the boy giggled.

"Sometimes, Jim, we all do things we wish we hadn't, like you when you used my car as part of your play. Afterward, you wished you hadn't done it. Isn't that true?"

Jamey nodded sheepishly.

"That happens to grown-ups, too, sometimes. But your dad's gone now and he can't ever make right things he probably wishes he hadn't done, like you did by cleaning the car again. If he was still around, I'll bet your dad would be awfully proud of how tall you've grown and what a smart kid you are. He's going to miss all the growing up you have left to do."

Hank stood and bent once more to clean off the

remaining water streaks. "I guess I feel kind of sorry for him," he said at last.

And I guess that says it all, Hank thought wryly in a moment of unexpected insight. For Marina, who could only take love, but never give it. For my grandmother, who lived to clean and so drove away her daughter and alienated her only living grandchild. All the joy they thoughtlessly threw away. When you got right down to it, Hank just felt sorry for them.

"Yeah. Me, too," Jamey said, industriously shining a hubcap. "Hank?"

"Yes, Jim?"

"You know when we were playing baseball yesterday?"

"Yes, Jim?"

"I was pretending you were my dad."

Hank's hand stilled for a long moment. "Now that's interesting, Jim." He slid the chamois over one last water spot. "I was pretending you were my son."

Hank, Gloria and Jamey left the Flannigan ranch just after lunch for the long drive back to Tulaca. Once on the paved surface of the main highway Gloria leaned back against the headrest of the Buick with a little sigh.

She felt tired and drained and disheartened.

Disheartened. A good word, she thought wearily. Her heart surely had been taken from her, and with its departure had gone her courage. Was there anything so wasted or weakening as love given but not returned?

Tired of her thoughts, she sat up again only to have Hank tell her without inflection, "Might as well get some sleep, Glorie.'' He gave a backward nod, indicating the back seat. ''Jim is already out for the count.''

Gloria followed the direction of his nod and saw that Jamey was indeed fast asleep, one arm hanging over the seat so that his hand rested on the puppy napping in its box on the floor. She smiled to herself. Jamey had had the time of his life with the Flannigan children.

Once more she leaned her head against the back of the seat and tried to follow Hank's suggestion, but sleep wouldn't come. Instead she used the darkness behind her eyes as an attempt to shut out Hank's pervasive presence. Her hands itched to touch him, her body tingled with the desire to have his next to it, her mouth ached with wanting Hank's hard lips ravaging its softness.

More than anything, she wanted to cry, wanted to scream out her pain and loss like a fishwife to an uncaring heaven.

Without warning, the fist she had unknowingly made in her lap was covered and she felt the roughness of Hank's bandaged fingers against her own. She opened her eyes, almost afraid to look at him, but saw that his attention was on the road ahead.

''Did you really think I would hurt your boy, Glorie? You came after me with a broom.''

The words were so far from her thoughts that for a moment she gazed at Hank blankly. Then she clasped his hand without even being aware she did it.

''I didn't think, Hank,'' she said softly. ''I just reached and knew at once my mistake. I'm so sorry.

There's no one I'd be more willing to trust my son with than you.''

Hank's eyes left the road ahead as he turned to look at her. Then he swung his attention back to the road.

"Will you marry me, Glorie?"

The words came so casually it took her a moment to make sense of what he said. She snatched her hand from under his as if burned.

"Because I know you won't hit me or physically abuse my child?" she asked tartly. "That's hardly a reason for marriage, Hank.''

His eyes never left the road. "Perhaps not, but last night is bothering you, isn't it? You said you don't normally go in for casual sex.''

"And now you want to play the noble male and make an honest woman of me," she replied, forcing sarcasm. Had casual sex been all it was to him?

"You know better than that. I want you to marry me, that's all.''

Gloria caught her breath. That's all? It sounded like a whole lot to her. "Why?" she asked baldly, striving to keep her own voice as collected as his.

"The usual reasons. We get along well together. We're compatible in bed, to say the least." He stopped and for a heated moment, their eyes met as each of them remembered. "Basically, we need each other.''

Gloria's heart stopped.

Hank quickly shifted his attention to the road again. "We both want a home," he continued, feeling as if he had no connection with the words at all. "We want sharing in our lives. I want children, and Jim is a boy to be proud of. I wouldn't mind if he's the only one, but he might like to have brothers and sisters."

The most important reason was conspicuous by its absence.

"Those aren't needs. Those are wants," Gloria replied tartly, fighting disappointment. "Don't you think being around the Flannigans has perhaps added a touch of envy to the initial frustration?" She knew she treaded a minefield, but didn't care if he blew up in her face. Anything to stop this farcical conversation.

He flicked her a curious glance from the corner of his eye. "Envy, yes. But where does the frustration come in?"

"You called Jane's name several times when you had the flu," she told him woodenly.

"And did you also hear Joaquin's name when I was being so chatty?"

Gloria flushed, feeling foolish. "Yes. At the time, I didn't know they were married. You just sounded as if Jane were someone special."

"She is, but not that way. Well, what do you think?"

"You would marry without love?"

He should have known he couldn't avoid that word.

"Love didn't do either of us any good the first time," he replied slowly. The word *affection* suddenly sounded pretty tepid. "I like you a lot," he said instead. "And surely you aren't a romantic, not after your first marriage, Glorie."

She leaned her head back against the seat, staring through half-lowered lashes at the highway stretching endlessly ahead. "Actually, I am. Perhaps even more so because of that marriage. I like you, too, Hank, but when I marry again, *if* I marry again," she said slowly, "I want to know that the man I've chosen loves me. And needs me."

Love. And need.

There was no sound for long moments but the low, powerful hum of the car.

Hank stared straight ahead, his mouth grim. "You want a man's soul," he replied at last.

"Does loving cost a man that much?"

Hank glanced at her impatiently. "You ask for love and need. Once you've got that, you also have a man's pride. So what does that leave him?" He answered his question bitterly before she could answer. "Nothing. And for what? A bed partner and an income tax deduction."

Immediately she bristled. "My man will have my love," she said tartly. "Love for love. Need for need. Pride for pride. What's so wrong with that, Hank Mason?"

But he remained stubbornly silent so that she changed the subject completely. "Jane said you're Joaquin's partner in F and M Trucking. What are you doing working at Johnny Holt's garage?"

Some of the tenseness left Hank's shoulders. He couldn't give Glorie what she wanted but he could give her money, something just as good. "Taking a rest. I go back to Tulaca every few years when life gets crazier than even I can manage."

He paused and took a breath, but couldn't bring himself to look at her. "I'm a wealthy man, Glorie. Joaquin and I are partners, but I also own the Mason Auto Parts chain. You might be familiar with it. And of course Johnny Holt Garages are mine. They're a chain now, too, but the one in Tulaca was my first business. I bought out Johnny's dad and licensed the name. Like your talent with computers, I found I had a talent for wheeling and dealing."

Now he glanced at her from the corner of his eye. Glorie looked straight ahead, her profile composed. He wanted her more than he'd ever wanted anyone or anything in his life. If she would just take what he had to offer.

"We'll have to disagree about love and need, but honest liking can be just as honorable...and just as stable. You also might want to consider that by marrying me, Glorie, you will be financially secure for life. Think about the advantages. Pretty clothes, travel. No problem with money for Jim to go to college someday."

"And what, besides a bed partner and two or more income tax deductions, do *you* get for your money, Hank?"

Her phrasing left him with a hollow, sinking feeling.

"I get a home," he said, "and a family." He sought for something to add to that short list but couldn't come up with anything. Everything else he wanted took barter of a different kind in an area where he wasn't spending.

Silence hung in the luxurious confines of the car for long moments, the only sound the low powerful hum of its motor.

"My lawyer forwarded Eric's insurance checks last week," Gloria said finally. "Between what I've put into savings and what I've set aside for investing, neither Jamey nor I should ever want for money again."

She turned slightly to examine Hank's hard, un-yielding profile, recognizing his mask now when she saw it. Home and family, he said. She of all people knew how important those two elemental concepts were.

Her hand fluttered for a moment. She wanted so badly to touch him, to kiss his mask away and fill his life and heart with all the love she and Jamey had so much of.

His offer was tempting, a temptation that set her heart pounding sluggishly. But she *wouldn't* sell to him. It was even trade or nothing.

Her hand settled on the seat beside her.

"I've already had a man give me everything you're offering, Hank, and it wasn't enough. You see, I've never been happier than I've been in the last couple of months, working in Mom's Café, put-tering around my ugly little house with its wonderful view of your mountain, and watching my son heal." She swallowed painfully, determined not to cry.

A muscle leapt in his jaw, but Hank's features didn't change.

"Well, Glorie," he said after a moment, "I'll ad-mit to being disappointed. I'd like to have been Jim's dad. He makes a great fishing partner."

He looked at her then, and smiled, the first smile he'd ever given her that didn't lighten and soften his features. She hoped she never received another like it.

"You'll get over it," she said with a small laugh to cover the bleakness in her voice, "and thank me one of these days. I'm saving you from endless base-ball games, football games, homework, and teacher conferences."

Sounds like a real horror show, all right, Hank thought. One for which he'd trade anything.

Okay. *Almost* anything.

Gloria put her head back against the seat and after a while went to sleep.

Chapter Eleven

Gloria decided not to give up her job at Mom's. As she told Hank, she was happy there. She enjoyed cooking and the interaction with the customers, most of whom lived in Tulaca. Jamey, too, needed to be around people and he was now as comfortable at Mom's as he was at home.

But most of all, Gloria knew she didn't want to spend long hours during the day with nothing but Hank Mason to occupy her mind. The nights were bad enough.

Hank was avoiding her.

He and Johnny Holt often took a coffee break at the café and the two men talked and joked in the laconic understated way of Western men. But now Hank seldom gave Gloria more than a passing greeting as she served their coffee.

Oh, he wasn't obvious about it. Nothing so crude as that, and no one but herself appeared to notice.

Perhaps, she thought in the early morning hours when sleep again eluded her, he treated her as he always had, but now the rapport, between them almost from the beginning, was missing. The man inside the granite mask had removed himself from her, and how she missed him! She'd never realized how many small emotional comforts he had given so freely, how much reliance she placed on that special look of his that told her she was a good mother...and a desirable woman.

A couple of times he took Jamey fishing, and once to a baseball game in Jakerville, but he picked the boy up while Gloria was working. When he brought him home in the evenings he merely let Jamey out of the car without getting out himself, waving to Gloria casually before driving off again when she appeared at the door to greet her son. He had the Thunderbird now, but she had no idea when he'd made the return trip to the Flannigans' to switch cars.

Mom Blackwell returned, bringing two of her grandchildren to spend time with their grandparents before school started. She assured Gloria that her job was safe.

She was tired of cooking, Mom said comfortably over an afternoon cup of coffee, and wanted time to enjoy her grandchildren. She was ready for younger hands to take over her work in the café for a while. Of course she would help out in emergencies and peak periods, and wasn't it nice that Jamey had someone to play with now?

Giving Gloria a motherly pat, she went to check

with her husband on the grocery order for the following day.

Gloria, watching Jamey run and shout with Mom's grandchildren on the Blackwells' lawn, could only agree.

Jamey had finally come into his own in the months they'd been in Tulaca. Gone was the silent, withdrawn child subject to hysterical tantrums. Now his small face glowed with health, sunshine, and self-confidence. Shyness might be a part of his personality, but it was no longer the result of fear or anxiety.

Hank's doing, of course, as everything good in their lives was Hank's doing. Jamey needed him so, and God help her, so did she.

Had she known how empty her life would be without him, would she have turned down his offer of marriage? If she went to him now, would he allow her to change her mind?

Gloria's hand paused in the act of filling the sugar containers that sat on each table. Dear heaven, what was she thinking! Hadn't one broken marriage taught her that relationships based on weakness crippled everything they touched?

And then came a week when Hank didn't come in at all.

After the first couple of days of Hank's absence, Gloria debated whether to ask Johnny about it, but in the end decided Tulaca had enough grist for its gossip mill.

The nights, which had been horrible, became terrible.

Friday evening of the week from hell arrived at last. Jamey was spending the night at the Blackwells'

to be up early the following morning to go with
Mom's grandchildren to the Jakerville zoo. Gloria
greeted the prospect of her free weekend with the
same enthusiasm as a trip to the dentist.

As she tidied the back counter in preparation for
the weekend's closing, she thought of her empty tomorrow…and of her empty tonight. In spite of willing the creeping second hand to slow even further, it
was almost eight o'clock. Time to go home.

Why? she wanted to ask the universe in general.
There's nothing at home for me when my family
isn't there.

The small house no longer charmed her. Now,
whenever her eyes roamed over its cheerful coziness,
she could only wish Hank were there to share it with
her, wish that she could make the house into a place
of warmth and love for him and banish forever his
bitter memories of it.

Perhaps she should find another house, she
thought, one without a front window view of Hank's
mountain. Or perhaps she should leave Tulaca altogether. She wiped a cloth over a tray and stacked it
with others under the counter. Wouldn't her heart
stand a better chance of recovery if she wasn't reminded of Hank every day?

Reaching behind her, she untied the apron protecting her dress. Leaving Hank would devastate Jamey, but in the long run, wouldn't it be for the best?

"You go along, Gloria," Mom told her from the
cash register where she was balancing the tape with
the meal checks. "Pop and I will lock up. You have
a good lazy weekend, dear, and rest up. You've been
looking kind of peaky lately."

Gloria smiled. Mom was aptly called, for she

mothered everyone who came into her small orbit, and Gloria and Jamey had become her special projects.

True to her prediction, she was fighting another sleepless night when there was a knock on her door in the small hours of the morning.

Jamey. Oh, God. Something had happened.

Heart beating fearfully, she stumbled to the front door.

It was Hank. And her heart stopped beating at all.

"Are you all right? W-what's wrong?"

Her greeting was a good sign, Hank thought, but this mission called for his best cool. "Nothing's wrong," he replied. "I was playing poker at Wade's but now the T-Bird won't start and I need daylight to see what's wrong. Do you mind if I stay here till morning? I'll sleep in the car," he tacked on in case she had misgivings.

She hesitated and Hank's face closed. "Forget it." He turned away. "Sorry I woke you."

Gloria reached out and caught his arm. "Come in."

"Are you sure, Glorie?" he asked, suddenly feeling foolish, standing on the woman's porch like a supplicant at three in the morning.

The same question he'd asked at the Flannigans' before his loving had described heaven to her, she thought, and nodded. "Yes, Hank. I'm sure."

Still not looking at her, Hank raised an arm and a car waiting at the curb drove off. Gloria hadn't realized it was there. Another rumor for the Tulaca grapevine, she thought fatalistically. Not that she gave one continental damn.

"How did the T-Bird get here?" she asked, seeing it parked in her driveway.

"A couple of buddies towed it home for me."

Home. The textbook Freudian slip. Hank could have kicked himself.

But Glorie's soft sigh whispered into the night before she repeated, "Come in," and he stepped from the porch into the house where he'd lived as a child, but that was never then his home.

He should have just gone ahead and gotten the car running at Wade's, he thought. With a good light, it wouldn't have been difficult. But the opportunity to come to Glorie again was too tempting to resist.

For a week he'd given it the good fight, and learned what unmitigated hell life without Glorie was like. Love for love was the coinage she demanded. Need for need. Even-steven. It had taken the week without her to make him realize that he would trade whatever it took. His soul, if need be. But what if Glorie had only friendship to offer in return? After all, she'd only said she *liked* him. Yet Joaquin said Glorie more than liked him.

What if Joaquin was wrong?

Stalemate. He felt like he was in junior high.

Well, fate and the T-Bird had given him the opportunity to come to her one more time. The only way to find out the extent of Glorie's feelings was to tell her the extent of his. It was now or never.

Hank pushed a hand through his hair, ruffling it, and Gloria hid a smile. He'd come to her, she thought exultantly, when he could have spent the night with anyone. "Home," he'd called her house. Had she ever received a greater compliment?

Searching for something to say, Hank's thoughts

stalled. He needed a lead-in of some sort. "Glorie, why did you let me into your house at three in the morning? With some men, that's not a very smart thing to do." There, that should get some kind of personal response and give him a clue as to what she felt for him.

Gloria slowly raised her face to his. Three o'clock in the morning. The hour when one confronts the past, he'd once said. Hank had needed her then.

But he hadn't moved from his position near the door. In another man she would have thought him poised for flight.

God, how she loved him!

"You're not just any man," she said, and his heart leapt, only to die a little when she added, "You've helped me out so many times. Why shouldn't I help you out, too?"

Empty, useless words, she thought, when what she wanted to do was throw her arms around him in joyous welcome. Had the man no idea he carried her heart in his hands?

Apparently not.

Hank answered her in a voice cold as a Siberian winter. "I help you out. You help me out. Don't you think we should be even by now? Even-steven, as the saying goes. Kaput. Quits."

Gloria stared at him blankly. What was he talking about? There was something in his voice she wasn't catching. "Don't be silly," she said at last.

But Hank had had enough. "Forget it. I'll sleep in the car." He turned toward the door. In doing so, he brushed against a small table and sent it crashing to the floor. The vase on it lay in pieces, two red roses in its watery debris.

He swore softly and righted the table, before bending to pick up the fragments of glass. "Sorry," he mumbled, his tone belligerent but a faint tinge of red across his high cheekbones.

Gloria, feeling shattered herself, reached down and picked up the two flowers. Mom Blackwell had given them to her the day before from one of her bushes. She touched a velvet petal gently, fighting a vision of moonlit shadows, wondering if roses brought Hank the same memories.

But memories and roses were forgotten when she stole a glimpse of his face.

A look of guilty vulnerability shadowed the hard features and tight mouth, the incongruously long and curling lashes were twin crescents against the high-planed cheekbones as he picked up fragments of the vase piece by piece and placed them in one large hand.

In his face she saw Jamey before they had come to Tulaca, before they had met a man named Hank Mason. How many times had this child-that-was been berated, or worse, in this very house for breaking something with small-boy carelessness?

As her soft laughter cut across the strained silence, Hank's lashes flicked up instantly.

She held her grin. "The vase isn't a family heirloom, Hank. Stop looking so reverent, as if it held the ashes of Great-Uncle Chester. I bought it for a quarter at a garage sale."

He wouldn't know she lied.

Jamey had proudly bought the vase at Bigelow's Mercantile for her with his first real allowance and Gloria treasured it, but there was no way on earth she would tell Hank that. Not when he smiled at her now, his eyes soft and crinkling nicely in the corners. She could get another tomorrow just like the broken one. Jamey would never know.

She's lying, Hank thought. Jim had told him about buying his mother the vase. Glorie was just trying to spare his feelings...*caring* again.

He sighed to himself. Might as well give it up, Mason. Some women are just like that. This one wasn't ever going to change. A man couldn't ask for a better *friend*.

Though he smiled wryly down into her upturned face, a bitterness behind Hank's eyes chilled Gloria. The smile slid from her features and she turned away, the ache to hold him and be held in return a painful thing.

In the kitchen Hank dropped the glass fragments into the trash can, then took the wad of paper toweling from her hand before she could return to the living room to clean up the water. "I'll do that. You go to bed. Like I said, I'll sleep in the car."

"It's going to rain," Gloria said quickly. "I've seen lightning. I think you should stay in the house."

Heat lightning. He knew damn well it wasn't going to rain, but what the hell. "Perhaps you're right," he agreed.

"The couch is too short for you. I'll use it and you can have the bed."

There. That should let him know she wasn't expecting bedroom games. Not, however, that she would turn them down tonight should they come her way.

"Are you being sacrificial again, Glorie?" Hank asked silkily, and Gloria clamped her mouth shut.

Damn him! Did he have to take everything and

twist it? His back was to her as he squatted to clean the water from the floor and for a moment she contemplated putting her tongue out at him, but changed her mind, settling for closing the bedroom door with a bang that rattled the windows.

Hank's low laughter filtered through the thin walls.

She heard him moving around for a few minutes before the door to the bedroom opened. Her heart stopped. But Hank was only going into the bathroom where in seconds she heard the lavatory tap running. Soon he was out, to walk through the bedroom again and close the door behind him. The light showing under the door went off. The little house grew quiet.

Gloria sighed. She really would have to leave Tulaca and the mountain that loomed over the small town so protectively. She couldn't stay. The pain of loving Tulaca's gentle mountain man would give her no peace.

Suddenly the bedroom door opened again and she saw the dim shape of Hank's bulk come in and move silently around to the opposite side of the bed. She felt the mattress depress under his weight and gave a soft sigh of relief as he lay down.

"You're right. The couch is too short," he explained softly. "Where's Jim?"

"Spending the night at the Blackwells'."

The words hung in the darkened bedroom provocatively for long moments, Hank's body acting on them immediately. But the heat died almost as soon as it was born.

A trade-off of good deeds, she'd said. So now he knew.

He didn't speak again, nor did Gloria, and he didn't touch her. Though still in his jeans and lying on top of the sheets, Hank's presence beside her on the bed brought comfort. She wanted to lie in his arms, but a woman can't always have everything. She'd take, for the time being, what she could get. Within moments, she slept.

Gloria awoke on his side of the bed late the next morning after sleeping deeply and dreamlessly for the first time in weeks. And she knew, because her absolute contentment told her so, that she'd slept in Hank Mason's arms.

He was gone. He'd made coffee and left a note on the kitchen table propped against the glass of water in which she had put the pair of roses.

Thanks. One word, no signature...and now only one rose in the glass.

Gloria drank her coffee, staring sightlessly at the crimson petals of the remaining flower. "Quits," he'd said. She had a sick feeling. ·

As she walked to the mercantile later that morning to replace the vase, she saw Johnny Holt across the street, coming out of the office to his garage. Ordinarily, Johnny closed on Saturdays and, on impulse, Gloria crossed the street to talk to him.

He watched her approach warily.

"Hello, Johnny."

"Gloria." The man nodded his head with a brevity bordering on rudeness.

"I...I wanted to talk to you about Hank."

"What about him?" Johnny turned his back on her and locked the door to the office.

Gloria continued doggedly. "I'm worried about him. He's acting...strange. Do you know why?"

Johnny turned on her a look of such unmitigated disgust that she stepped back a pace.

"I owe Hank a hell of a lot, lady, but I don't owe you a damn thing and I don't talk behind a friend's back. If you want answers, you ask him!"

His eyes narrowed even farther. "When Hank needs a rest from his business interests, he comes to Tulaca for it. This is his town, not yours. A few weeks ago he was talking about moving down here permanent. Now all of a sudden he's leavin' for Albuquerque today and doesn't know when he'll be back. Thanks to you, prob'ly."

Johnny glared at her, making no attempt to hide his animosity, and Gloria's mind reeled as she tried to assimilate what the man hurled at her.

All she could really understand, however, was that Hank intended to leave Tulaca and Johnny Holt blamed her for it.

"Loan me your car," she ordered abruptly.

"Now you wait just a minute, missy. I don't—"

Gloria drew herself up and stared the little man straight in the eye. "I'm going up the mountain," she said, "and I'll have things straight with Hank by the time I get off. If I don't," she added, seeing Johnny weaken, "he won't have to leave Tulaca. I will. Is it a deal?"

Johnny gave her a long, speculative look, assessing the woman's wild silken hair, her high aristocratic cheekbones and sensitive mouth under golden-flecked brown eyes glittering now with determination. Feature by feature they weren't much, but together they added up to a formidable beauty.

For a moment he saw the same element of danger he glimpsed from time to time in Hank's eyes. Those two were a pair, all right.

He gave a curt nod. "It's a deal." He fished in

his pocket for the keys. "You can drive a four-on-the-floor Firebird Trans Am, can't you?" he asked, hesitating a moment before handing them to her.

"I can drive anything on four wheels," Gloria said shortly, and took the keys from him before he could change his mind. "I'll get it back to you without a scratch."

"Good luck to you then," Johnny said, but added warningly, "I mean what I say."

Gloria merely nodded and settled herself in the low, sleekly shining, black sports car with its golden firebird insignia splayed proudly over the hood.

Under the open sunroof her hair glinted blue-black in the strong sunlight.

Johnny Holt didn't loan his car casually. Though the Trans Am wasn't new, it was already a classic of its kind and Johnny's wife and Hank Mason only just nudged the car out of the running for being the love of his life.

Yet watching it roar off down the main street of Tulaca under the Pellman woman's expert handling, he had the uncomfortable conviction the wrong person owned it. The woman and car were a perfect match.

Gloria parked behind the Thunderbird in Hank's meadow and walked on shaky legs to the cabin. The heavy wooden door stood open but the cabin was quiet. When she knocked on the screen, no one answered.

Opening it, she stepped inside. A small valise stood near the door. Hank was leaving.

The empty cabin already seemed to bear the stamp of desertion—spotlessly clean, the bed stripped of its linens, the fireplace swept, no dishes left out in the kitchen area. Except on the table. There, Flintstone characters cavorted around a jelly glass filled with water.

In it was the other rose.

Hank strode through the trees for a last few minutes at the cliff.

It was time. His bag was packed, the cabin clean.

Albuquerque had kept Johnny's telephone so busy for the last couple of weeks that the garage customers were having a difficult time getting through. The gist of most of those calls was that if he didn't get his tail back in harness pretty soon all his hard work before leaving in the first place was going down the tube.

He stood now at the cliff edge and gazed at the familiar vista of sky and mountains. His old friend, the eagle, coasted on a convenient air current checking out the terrain far below.

Earth and air.

On one side of him stood a grief-stricken, seven-year-old boy who wanted a woman's arms to hold him as he cried out his loss and fear. At his other side, tall, gangly, and awkward, was a fifteen-year-old boy thrust into abrupt manhood with the sudden realization that he was exchanging acts of kindness for the illusion of love.

The three of them stood shoulder to shoulder, invincible. It would take a formidable opponent to even think of breaking up their solidarity...except when confronted by one small wild-haired woman.

Earth and air.

Hank suddenly threw his head back. He was

through, by damn, of letting the ghost of a golden-eyed warrior princess drive him off his mountain. Never again. And he sure as hell wasn't taking the woman's ghost with him to Albuquerque.

He was taking the real thing.

Glorie Pellman was going to be a permanent part of his life if he had to drag her into it kicking and screaming. He'd never been good at beating around the bush and he should have known he couldn't do it with Glorie. If he had to say the words first and straight out, he'd say them. *I love you.* Not a gutless *affection.* Not a lukewarm *like,* but I...love...you. It couldn't be that hard.

Why had he doubted that she loved him? He knew she did. It had been written all over her for weeks, ever since they'd come back from the Flannigans'. When he'd asked her why she let him in last night, she might have mouthed all that you-helped-me-out nonsense, but her golden eyes had told another tale. His Glorie was such a lousy liar.

Love for love. Need for need. Pride for pride. He could live with that.

In his mind, Hank turned to the small lost boy he'd been. Go home, he said. There's a woman there to kiss your nightmares away and a towheaded youngster to play with. A cliff edge is no place for a kid your size.

With a relief Hank felt clear to his heart, the child went.

There are things one person just does for another, Joaquin had said.

Did you hear that, boy? Hank asked his teenage self. Take all the hugs and Christmas boxes you can get. Give 'em back when you can. That's called living. It's lonesome on this mountain. Get back to Tulaca and have a ball.

As the youth departed, Hank mentally called after him, And when you find the right partner, don't keep score. Remember that, boy.

He turned...and found his Glorie just coming through the trees behind him, eyes blazing.

She met him halfway and stopped to fling out, "I have a question."

Hank wanted to laugh, but he knew better. God, he loved this woman. "What is it, Glorie?" he asked with what he knew to be infuriating mildness.

"Do you love me?"

It stopped him cold. He opened his mouth, but for a moment nothing came out so he closed it again. It would have been nice if she'd given him time to practice.

She saw his jaw tighten and a nerve jump spasmodically along its rigid line. She took another step forward.

He tried to buy time by asking, "Did you walk all the way up here just to ask me that?"

"I didn't walk. I have Johnny Holt's car."

Hank's brows rose in a small show of admiration. "I'm impressed. Johnny doesn't usually loan his Trans Am."

Glorie stared at him, unblinking. "Don't change the subject. Do you love me? Words of one syllable will do. Yes or no?"

Swallowing, he again opened his mouth, only to have his words die unborn. Who would have thought this would be so damn difficult? And of course Glorie jumped right into the wrong conclusion.

"You coward," she said witheringly, then suddenly shouted so that a bird flew up with a startled cry somewhere in the trees, "You do love me, damn you, just as much as I love you but you're too damned lily-livered to say it!"

There had to be a lot of Western movies in her past, Hank thought with a silent chuckle of relief as he reached for her.

But she knocked his reaching arms away to snarl, "This mountain isn't enough, is it? That's why you're going. Messing with your blasted motors doesn't get me out of your system, either, does it?"

She glared at him through the first real tears he'd ever seen her cry and pushed at his chest with a stiff forefinger, causing him to step back a pace. "Oh no, heart-of-stone Hank Mason is too tough to say he l-loves anyone," she spluttered. "You're like that eagle out there—" she flung out a hand that just missed striking him "—so far above the rest of us who l-love and c-care. Well, I hope you and your eagle are v-very h-happy together." With that, she spun on her heel to leave Hank to his aerie.

Hard hands took her shoulders, their grip gentle but firm. She struggled wildly, the sobs tearing out of her now as Hank pulled her back against his chest. But when she felt the strength of his muscled body against her back, she stopped struggling, knowing she couldn't win. Her head bowed forward in defeat as she fought now to suppress the hated tears, but the hands on her shoulders turned her inexorably around.

"Since when is Glorie Pellman such a big crybaby?"

Her head jerked up and she glared at him, eyes molten.

Hank smiled. "That's better." With a calloused palm he rubbed the tears from each side of her belligerent face, then gently smoothed the damp hair from her heated cheeks.

"I want to show you something," he said as he turned her stiff body to the side to face the sky-filled vista beyond the cliff, his arm a pleasant weight across her shoulders.

She shrugged irritably, testing, but the weight remained.

"Do you see that eagle out there?"

Gloria scowled, refusing to answer. She hated eagles.

"He's not really alone, you know. He has a nest back over the mountain with eaglets to feed. You can bet Mrs. Eagle is near it somewhere."

She tried to pull away, but the arm around her wouldn't let her go.

"Eagles mate for life," Hank informed her quietly.

Breathing suspended, she stilled.

"You said I'm like that bird out there. I wish it were true. It would be nice to know that as I went about my day-to-day business someone at home waited for me. He needs Mrs. Eagle quite badly, you know." Hank's drawl held a rare uncertainty. "Without her and the brood, his hunting has no real meaning and he knows it."

"Don't forget Mrs. Eagle," Gloria said huskily, her eyes now focused on the bird hanging so majestically in the sky, carrying all her dreams. "She needs him just as much and the eaglets need them both.''

''Actually, that may be Mrs. Eagle,'' Hank replied with a touch of dry humor. ''At this distance it's hard to tell. They're very alike, except in size.''

He turned her so that she faced him, his arms remaining across her shoulders. ''I...I do, uh, love you,'' he said, stumbling badly, but at least he got the words out this time.

Gloria shrugged off his arm. Did he think he owed her that just because she'd thrown away her pride and chased up his mountain after him? ''Big of you, I'm sure. I love you more. So?''

We should be riding off into the sunset about now, Hank thought. What the hell was the problem? He'd said the words. She'd said the words. The End. ''So I need you,'' he growled.

She glowered at him. ''I need you more.''

Slowly, Hank began to smile. ''You do?''

''I do.''

''That kind of has a nice ring to it, don't you think?'' he asked, so softly she had to lean forward right into his waiting arms to hear it.

''I do,'' she whispered while she still could.

Later they walked back through the trees, Gloria snugged fast under Hank's arm.

''Say it again, Hank, and this time don't stutter.''

He grinned. ''I love you, Glorie, my glory.''

''Beautiful,'' she whispered. ''I love you, too, Hank, so very very much.''

They had to stop to express the words in another language, then resumed walking.

''Is Jim still at Mom's?'' Hank asked casually.

Gloria's answer was just as casual. "Mmm-hmm."

"Think he'll be all right there for a while?"

"Mmm-hmm."

They walked through the cabin door. "How did you like my feather pillows last time you slept over?" he asked provocatively, leading her deliberately toward the bed.

"Luxury personified. I liked your mattress, too." Keeping her mouth prim, Gloria planted her rear end firmly on the mattress under discussion.

Hank leaned over to capture her mouth with his.

Prim melted into blatantly parted.

After long satisfying moments, he raised his hand just long enough to growl, "You're marrying me, aren't you?"

"Oh, my. Most certainly," Gloria said and pulled Hank's hand down again.

"Know what size bed we're going to have in the great big house I've got in Albuquerque?" he muttered roughly against her seeking tongue, then jumped because his zipper was being slowly but most certainly unzipped.

"Mmm?" Gloria asked.

Hank undid her front buttons one by one. "The same size bed we have in this itty-bitty cabin," he replied huskily. "Double. Just big enough for two. We'll have to sleep—" his hand cupped a breast "—close."

"You read my mind," Gloria whispered, throwing her head back to give Hank's lips easier access to the pulse beating just under her ear.

Small teeth nipped his male nipple as he bent over her, and his whole body spasmed. "That's why...we're t-two of a k-kind,'' he managed to get out with the last oxygen in his lungs.

Gloria wanted to tell him he was stuttering again, but she couldn't. She had no breath left at all.

So there was one sure way to keep his glory from having the last word, Hank thought before his brain stopped and love took over completely. Keep her breathless.

He'd see to it.

* * * * *

SILHOUETTE

> SPECIAL EDITION ®

COMING NEXT MONTH

TEXAS BABY Joan Elliott Pickart

That's My Baby! & Family Men

Margaret Madison had decided to become a mother again at forty-six. Little Alison needed her. But Gibson McKinley, the man Margaret had just fallen for, didn't even want to remarry, let alone become a daddy!

A DADDY FOR DEVIN Jennifer Mikels

Rugged homicide cop Riley Garrison still hungered for the love he'd forsaken two years ago, but then he came upon Allie again. Allie and her fatherless sixteen-month-old...

THE COWBOY'S BRIDE Cathy Gillen Thacker

Hasty Weddings

Thanks to his clever, cunning uncle, Cody was going to have to remarry his runaway bride, but this time he was definitely going to have his wedding night!

BROTHER OF THE GROOM Judith Yates

Holly West had fled town after being left at the altar and no one had ever known that she was carrying her fiancé's child...

THE COP AND THE CRADLE Suzannah Davis

Switched at Birth

Jake Lattimer's newly discovered twin brother had dumped his burned-out partner on him and she was driving Jake nuts! This lady cop was nosy and, what was worse, she was dreaming of adding to the Lattimer family tree...

THE MILLIONAIRE'S BABY Phyllis Halldorson

Kate had no idea that the man she'd rescued was millionaire Burk Sinclair, nor did she know what he would do when he realised that she, 'the enemy', was carrying his child.

Available at most branches of WHSmith, John Menzies, Martins, Tesco, Asda, Volume One, Sainsbury, Safeway and other good paperback stockists

COMING NEXT MONTH FROM

SILHOUETTE®

Intrigue
Danger, deception and desire

A REAL ANGEL Cassie Miles
LITTLE GIRL LOST Adrianne Lee
THE ABANDONED BRIDE Jane Toombs
FAMILY TIES Joanna Wayne

Desire
Provocative, sensual love stories for the woman of today

LOOK WHAT THE STORK BROUGHT Dixie Browning
THE HAND-PICKED BRIDE Raye Morgan
BIG SKY DRIFTER Doreen Owens Malek
WIFE FOR A NIGHT Carol Grace
TALL, DARK AND TEMPORARY Susan Connell
MARRIAGE ON HIS MIND Susan Crosby

Sensation
A thrilling mix of passion, adventure and drama

THE AMNESIAC BRIDE Marie Ferrarella
LOVE WITH THE PROPER STRANGER Suzanne Brockmann
MARRYING JAKE Beverly Bird
WIFE, MOTHER...LOVER? Sally Tyler Hayes

On sale in August 1998

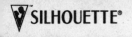

ORD INK

We are giving away a year's supply of Silhouette® books to the five lucky winners of our latest competition. Simply fill in the ten missing words below, complete the coupon overleaf and send this entire page to us by 31st January 1999. The first five correct entries will each win a year's subscription to the Silhouette series of their choice. What could be easier?

BUSINESS	**SUIT**	CASE
BOTTLE	_____	HAT
FRONT	_____	BELL
PARTY	_____	BOX
SHOE	_____	PIPE
RAIN	_____	TIE
ARM	_____	MAN
SIDE	_____	ROOM
BEACH	_____	GOWN
FOOT	_____	KIND
BIRTHDAY	_____	BOARD

Please turn over for details of how to enter ⇨

C8G

HOW TO ENTER

There are ten words missing from our list overleaf. Each of the missing words must link up with the two on either side to make a new word or words.

For example, 'Business' links with 'Suit' and 'Case' to form 'Business Suit' and 'Suit Case':

BUSINESS—SUIT—CASE

As you find each one, write it in the space provided. When you have linked up all the words, fill in the coupon below, pop this page into an envelope and post it today. Don't forget you could win a year's supply of Silhouette® books—you don't even need to pay for a stamp!

Silhouette Word Link Competition
FREEPOST CN81, Croydon, Surrey, CR9 3WZ
EIRE readers: (please affix stamp) PO Box 4546, Dublin 24.

Please tick the series you would like to receive if you are one of the lucky winners

Desire™ ❏   Special Edition™ ❏   Sensation™ ❏   Intrigue™ ❏

Are you a Reader Service™ subscriber?   Yes ❏   No ❏

Ms/Mrs/Miss/Mr ....Initials ....
(BLOCK CAPITALS PLEASE)

Surname..

Address ....

....

....Postcode.........................

(I am over 18 years of age)   G8C